Brown Sugar in Minnesota

COOPER SMITH BOOK 1

Joe Field

Published by Mesabi Range Publishing, Minnesota

CONTENTS

*This is for my beloved family
and the kindred spirits of the North Star State*

Chapter 1

Red Lake Indian Reservation, MN

It was a Friday night in early April when two hefty men
from Minneapolis walked into the front entrance of the Red
Lake Casino thirty miles north of Bemidji. Both men were in
their mid-thirties. They dressed and looked alike with
matching blue LA Dodgers caps angled to the side covering
short black hair. They had brown eyes, prominent noses, and
well-groomed beards from their favorite barber back home.
They wore long-sleeved shirts that looked two sizes too
small, baggy blue jeans held by thick leather belts, and
heavy-duty Carhartt boots. One man chewed a toothpick
while the other sucked down a cigarette. The man with the
cigarette was slightly taller, but the man with the toothpick
had a commanding presence about him. They swaggered
through the casino's lobby. They had been instructed to head
to the back of the casino floor for the slot machines with the
unmistakable picture of a redneck fisherman casting his rod
to catch walleye casino-tokens. They would buy a roll of
quarters, sit and play for a while, and wait for further
instructions.

The majority of the casino's clientele were retired
grandmas and grandpas spending their Social Security checks
on the only entertainment around. Most were too mesmerized
by their slot machines to notice the two strangers, but the
ones who did see them stared until their slots started spinning
again. The men found their designated machines and started

putting quarters in. They watched as the walleye aimlessly spun round and round.

After the third spin, the man with the cigarette leaned toward the other and said, "Hey, Jimmy, do you think we are the first two black guys to step foot in this casino or what?"

"No, but I'm pretty sure we're the only two black guys that grandma over there has ever seen," Jimmy replied, pointing at a casino wall mirror reflecting an old woman gawking at them from a slot machine across the room.

Both men snickered. "Are Smokey and Tank in position?" the man with the cigarette asked.

Jimmy checked his phone and nodded. "They are ready to go. Are you?"

"I'm ready," his partner said. "Let's just do it and get out of here. These Indian reservations give me a bad vibe."

"These reservations will make us all rich," said Jimmy. "So get used to them, and let me do the talking."

Just as the man with the cigarette won a small handful of quarters, two tribesmen marched over and stood behind them. Jimmy could see in the mirror that they were of equal size and stature to him and his partner, Marcus. If people thought Jimmy and Marcus were brothers or twins, then these two guys were either identical twins or doppelgangers. Jimmy guessed they were about forty years old. Their long black hair was tied tightly into ponytails behind clean-shaven faces that revealed several nasty scars. Most likely knife fights, thought Jimmy. The one standing behind Marcus wore a long-sleeved, maroon button-up shirt with a bolo tie featuring a red eagle medallion and two feathers. The one behind Jimmy wore a tight red V-neck t-shirt under a black suit jacket with a red bear pin.

"Are you the boys from the cities?" said the one with the tie on.

"Yes," answered Jimmy. He and Marcus turned their swiveling stools to face the men.

"My name is Jason Red Eagle," said the man with the tie.

"Let me guess, that makes you Mr. Red Bear, right?" Jimmy asked the other man, somewhat sarcastically.

"Yes. Matthew Red Bear, to be exact. How did you know…" His voice trailed off as Jimmy pointed to his pin.

"I'm Jimmy, and this is Marcus."

"Where are the others? We were told there would be four of you."

"Change of plans," said Jimmy. "Tell your boss that Smokey wants to meet him away from the casino so Grandma over there doesn't burn holes through us with her eyes." Jimmy pointed to the same woman who had been staring at him minutes before. "Or worse, we want to protect against the rare chance that you could be working with the police planning to get all of us on video making the deal." Jimmy gestured toward the security cameras on the ceiling.

"Going off-site wasn't part of the agreement," said Jason.

"Too bad," said Jimmy. "Either you get your boss and meet us outside by our vehicle, or we are out of here and you can kiss your profits goodbye." Jimmy motioned to Marcus and the two stood up and started to walk away.

"All right, hold on," said Jason. "Let me call my boss quick. You guys wait outside – we will be there soon."

"We are in the black Cadillac CTS in the northeast parking lot," said Jimmy.

"We know," said Jason and Matthew simultaneously, glancing up at one of the security cameras.

"See my point," said Jimmy. "We will wait five minutes, but not ten. So make it quick."

***

Exactly five minutes later, Jimmy and Marcus saw two red Ford pickup trucks heading straight for their car in the parking lot. Jason and Matthew were the drivers, and each truck had a passenger. Jason pulled up alongside the Cadillac with his window down, motioning for Jimmy to do the same.

"Follow us," said Jimmy, his window halfway down.

"Let's just do this here and be done with it," replied Jason, glancing nervously at his passenger.

It was dark, but Jimmy could see the second person in Jason's truck was wearing a cowboy hat, which meant he was the boss – a ruthless local drug-dealer named William Kingbird. "We are going to drive just a little east of here to get away from all the cameras and grandmas," said Jimmy. "It will only take us five minutes to get there."

Jason looked at his boss, who slowly nodded his head. "All right, let's go," said Jason.

The trucks followed close behind the Cadillac as the group headed out of the parking lot and continued east along the deserted old reservation highway. After four miles, the Cadillac slowed, its headlights beaming on a second black Cadillac, this one an Escalade. Smokey and Tank were inside, parked across the road perpendicular to a bridge spanning Little Rock Creek. Jimmy pulled his sedan up behind the Escalade, covering the remaining open section of the bridge. The trucks crept to within fifty feet of the Cadillacs and stopped. All eight men jumped out of their vehicles and met in the middle.

"Hello, Mr. Kingbird. It's nice to finally meet you in person," said Smokey in a booming voice. Smokey – whose real name was Tyrone Carter – had received his nickname because of his uncanny resemblance to Smokey the Bear. He was a big, lumbering thirty-eight-year-old just over six feet tall. His frame was solid muscle over a chubby core, similar to the physiques of NFL defensive linemen. He had a beard that covered almost every inch of his face and neck. He wore a black leather jacket, baggy blue jeans, and Carhartt boots. Smokey commanded respect from his employees and associates by his large personality and charismatic presence.

He was also known to be ruthless and unforgiving, although he had a softer, manipulative side, too.

"Hello, Smokey. It's nice to meet you, too," said Kingbird. "But why the last-minute change of plans?"

Smokey looked Kingbird over and noticed he looked every bit the stereotypical older native dressed in complete Western style, including the cowboy hat, Western button-down shirt, blue jeans, and cowboy boots. Kingbird was in his mid-fifties, and his long hair had a salt-and-pepper contrast to it. He wore glasses and was clean-shaven. He had a short, wiry frame and was well past his prime.

"Sorry about the change," said Smokey. "We need to be careful and discreet about our meetings. I am pleased, though, to be standing on the reservation owned by your proud Chippewa tribe. Hey, who is the kid?" Smokey motioned behind Kingbird.

"This here is my boy, William Kingbird, Junior," Kingbird said. The kid was a mirror image of his father, except that he looked around twenty years old. He even wore the same Western attire minus the cowboy hat. "He will be taking over the family business one day and should be included in these discussions. And these other two are my trusted employees, Jason Red Eagle and Matthew Red Bear."

"We look forward to working with you all," said Smokey. "These are my employees – Jimmy, Marcus, and Tank." Smokey had to point up when he said Tank's name. His nickname was well earned – he was built like a M4 Sherman. Tank was likely the largest black man to ever step foot on the Red Lake Indian Reservation. He had a shaved head, thick beard, and a giant nose. He wore a matching windbreaker jacket and pants, and custom-made tennis shoes.

"Pleased to meet you," said Kingbird. "Now, let's get down to business. You claim you can supply us with the purest heroin in the country. What's your secret?"

Smokey nodded. "Yes, we receive our opium from the best farms in Mexico via secret supply lines. I can import the goods safely without blemish to your reservation each month. We, of course, carry most of the risk, but our prices are still competitive. This allows our local dealers to turn a handsome profit. If you plan to deal for us, you must agree to provide our product to your customers in its most pure form. No dilutions. We call our product Brown Sugar. Think of it as the Rolls Royce of heroin."

"How much for a kilo?" asked Kingbird.

"One hundred thousand dollars," replied Smokey.

Kingbird shook his head. "One hundred K? I can get a kilo out east for $60,000 with no strings attached. I dilute that down to fifty percent purity and instantly double my profits."

"Yes, but your customers would be receiving a terrible product," Smokey countered. "Don't worry, though. We assume you'll dilute the product, so we cut the kilo for you and have the single-dose packages ready to sell. They even have our Brown Sugar label on them. You give the finished product to your street-level dealers, and they will sell it like hotcakes." Smokey smiled.

"This arrangement is not going to work for us," said Kingbird, raising his voice. "I've owned the drug market on this reservation for two decades, and I'm not about to cut my profits because a bunch of tough guys from the cities come up here and tell us they have a superior product. Our clientele doesn't care about a Rolls Royce – they want a Ford Pinto. A quick and cheap high."

"You're wrong, Mr. Kingbird. Your users will prefer our product once they try it because they will get the best high of their lives," Smokey insisted. "You there" – he jerked his head toward Jason. "Come over here and try a hit of Brown Sugar."

Jason glanced at his boss. Kingbird nodded his permission. Smokey pulled a small brown bag out of his inside coat pocket and handed it to Jason. Jason brought it to the rear of his truck. He poured the bag's brown contents down on a cutting board that he kept in a bin on his truck bed. He started to smash the heroin into a fine powder with the butt of his hunting knife.

As Jason prepared the heroin, Smokey's voice brought everyone's attention back to him. "Mr. Kingbird, Junior, and Matthew. I think the three of you really missed out here. This could have been a big day, but greed got the best of you."

Kingbird scowled. "What are you implying?"

"I'm just saying you guys missed the boat, or the canoe, or whatever the saying is up here on the res—"

Three loud bangs in rapid succession from Jason Red Eagle's assault rifle interrupted Smokey's words. Three well-placed rounds hit the upper spines of Matthew, Kingbird, and his son. They slammed face forward into the gravel. They were dead within seconds.

"Well done, Jason!" yelled Smokey. "We will have to start calling you Eagle Eye instead of Red Eagle from now on. Hurry up and help us throw the bodies into the creek so we can get out of here."

The dead were thrown off the bridge into Little Rock Creek, their bodies instantly lost in the darkness.

"Now that we have those guys out of the way, here is your territory acquisition bonus and first kilo of Brown Sugar for you to sell to the network," said Smokey, handing Jason a stack of bills bound together with rubber bands in one hand, and a duffle bag full of drugs in the other.

"I won't let you down, Smokey," Jason promised. "I will make you a lot of money up here."

"That's what I like to hear. Now, we need a solid forty-eight hours before anyone catches wind of what happened tonight. Do you think you can keep everything under wraps until Sunday night at least?"

"You can count on me."

Smokey shook Jason Red Eagle's hand, and the four black men got back into their Cadillacs and headed west to the next acquisition meeting on the White Earth Indian Reservation.

Chapter 2

Duluth, MN

The Smith family reunion was held every year on the Fourth of July weekend in Lester Park in East Duluth. The summer get-together started five years before I was born, so this year marked the big thirtieth annual family reunion. It was a summer highlight with eighty to ninety Smiths in attendance, depending on the birth-to-death ratio the preceding year. Several standard events took place during the day, including the water balloon toss competition, cliff jumping into the river, and the dreaded name-draw known in the family as "the decision". The decision consisted of placing the names of all the Smith family adults into a hat. Whoever had his or her name pulled was in charge of organizing the following year's event. My name had yet to be called since I became a legal adult. Last year my younger sister Jill's name was drawn, and she went all out this year. This included matching white t-shirts for everyone with the words *got smith?* in large black font on the front, and *30 years of milk mustaches* on the back. We are required to wear them around town all weekend and pretend not to be embarrassed.

Most of my family still lived in Duluth and would never leave, and I couldn't blame them. I looked around the park at our huge family and started counting the number of Smiths who had moved outside of Saint Louis County. Just as I looked down at my hand to actually total them up, I saw a whizzing football flying my direction. I instinctively brought my hands up and caught it before it crashed into my nose.

"Heads up, Coop," called my cousin, Jesse, two seconds later then he needed to.

"Hey, Jesse, nice throw," I said, tossing the ball back at him. "When did you start throwing the pigskin like a Sally? Had you thrown the ball like that back in high school, we would have lost every game."

"Lucky for you I didn't," said Jesse. "I made a Greyhound hero out of you at East High with all those touchdowns I threw you."

"That's true," I said, "but I had to make acrobatic catches every time you threw the ball!" I caught his next pass with one hand just for show.

Jesse and I were born just three days apart on the sixth and the ninth days of November, respectively, in 1989. Growing up, Jesse liked to remind me how young I was compared to him. I didn't mind being born after him – my birthday occurred on the same day as the fall of the Berlin Wall, which seemed fitting given my lifelong obsession with the news.

All of the many Smith cousins grew up playing sports and games together in the Woodland neighborhood of Duluth. Eventually, Jesse became the starting quarterback at Duluth East High School, with me as his go-to wide receiver. We set a Greyhound school record in 2006 for the most touchdowns thrown and received that year. We both had illusions of grandeur about playing ball in college, but it didn't work out for either of us. Seven years after high school, Jesse was still in decent shape. He was tall with an athletic build. He had sun tanned skin, brown hair, and blue eyes. He wore his *got smith?* shirt with black gym shorts and white sneakers.

"Does the Sheriff have a gym up in Bemidji to keep you deputies in shape?" I asked.

"Of course," said Jesse. "I'm still jacking steel after all these years. How about you – does MPR have a tough-guys gym down in Saint Paul?"

"Yeah, can't you tell?" I said as I flexed my muscles. Truth was, I hadn't kept in as good shape as Jesse after high school. I had stayed in Duluth and gone to journalism school at UMD, where the "freshman fifteen" quickly caught up with me. It took me three solid years of exercise to burn ten of the fifteen pounds off after college. I wasn't as muscular as I was back in high school, but I still had a solid build. At exactly six feet tall, I was shorter than most of my brothers and cousins, but what I lacked in height I made up for in speed and endurance in athletics. I was a true Irish redhead growing up, but thankfully my hair had gotten darker over the years and was more brown than red now. And I hid the freckles on my cheeks behind a scruffy red beard. I wore glasses now, and I was a freak about my teeth, which were so straight and white they were more fit for television than radio.

"Congratulations, by the way," said Jesse.

"For what?"

"For marrying up! Soojin seems great."

"Thanks. She is."

"Is she still practicing karate? I heard she can break thick pine boards like they are twigs."

"Yes, and she could break a guy's neck just as easily. I never thought I would marry someone who would fare better in a street fight than me."

"That's awesome. Say, Grace mentioned it the other day while I was distracted watching the Twins play, but when is the wedding again?"

"The first day of September, during Labor Day weekend. We figured the only way to get all of you to come to the cities would be to have our wedding take place on the heels of the Minnesota State Fair. And, of course, the Twins and the Vikings were playing in town."

"That was a good call. Count Grace and I in for sure," said Jesse, catching the football. "Well, at least for the ice-cold milk at the fair, and a corndog at Target Field."

"So, what have you been busy with up in Beltrami County these days? Anything you can share with a junior radio reporter trying to make a break in the big city?" I winked.

"Well, I can't go into specifics, but we have a real drug problem up there. It's getting out of control." Jesse tucked the ball under his arm and walked over to me.

"Really? What kind of drugs?"

"Mostly heroin and synthetic drugs like OxyContin."

"That's interesting."

"About three months ago, some big-time drug dealer came up from Minneapolis to the Red Lake Indian Reservation. He gunned down the local competition and started selling heroin. The users of the drug are calling it Brown Sugar. These addicts can't get enough of the stuff. Lab tests have proved it to be some of the purest heroin on the market right now."

"Sounds like something out of *Breaking Bad.* Were you able to arrest the dealer?"

"Unfortunately, no. This dealer then went over to the White Earth Indian Reservation and shot up the local competition near Mahnomen the following day. The DEA is involved, and they are working with law enforcement offices across the state."

"Are you and Grace going to be safe up there with all of this activity?"

"Yeah, all of Grace's family is still in Bemidji, and we feel safe. For now."

"That's good. I hope you guys stay safe." I paused, then added, "This sounds like it could be a story."

Jesse looked dubious, so before he could object, I added, "I haven't produced a big story yet at MPR. They have something called the 'Last-In-First-Out' policy. This means the last people hired are usually the first to go if they need to lay people off. There are rumors circulating at work about possible cuts – that is, unless you produce big enough stories to make that policy worthless. Is it okay with you if I do some more research on this drug network and see if I can turn it into my first noteworthy story?"

"Sure. But as you just pointed out, these guys are dangerous. You'll need to watch your back and let me or your brothers know if you are in trouble," said Jesse.

"Nothing to worry about, Jesse. You guys might all think you are indestructible with your badges and guns – but really I am the invincible one with my reporter credentials and voice recorder." I smiled. "Say, I think I see Soojin motioning for me to save her from Grandma Cece. Let's catch up later on this – I may pay you a visit up there at some point if this story gets legs."

"Sounds good – just don't go trying any of that Brown Sugar. They say if you try it even once, you'll never be able to stop."

***

I scampered over to rescue my future bride just as she flashed facial expressions that suggested Grandma Cece had overstepped some boundaries. Soojin Kim was the only child of Korean immigrants from Seoul who moved to Minnesota a year before Soojin's birth. Her father landed an engineering job with 3M, and they resettled in the Twin Cities suburb of Woodbury. Soojin's childhood was marred by the death of her mother when she was only seven years old. When she turned to her father, he focused her energies on martial arts. She ended up winning the USA Junior Taekwondo Championship three years in a row from 2004 to 2006.

Not only was she tough as nails, but Soojin had a beauty and charm that drew people to her. This worked wonders in her political work. She was a rising star in

Minnesota's DFL, and was currently working on the media team for Governor Knutson. She had helped Knutson get elected in a tight race back in 2010. People often remarked that it wouldn't be long before she would be running for office.

Soojin and I had bonded over liberal politics in the midst of our conservative families. We met when we were both volunteering at a DFL political fundraising event last year, and I was lucky enough to work the same registration booth as her. I tried to play it cool, but the butterflies in my stomach made me tongue-tied for most of the night. I finally asked her out as we were packing up, and she agreed. Thirteen months later, she was at her first Smith family reunion, and our wedding was in two short months.

As I drew closer, I heard Grandma Cece saying, "I know you work for Knuston, but I'm definitely voting for Nelson in November. You know *he* is pro-life and against gay marriage. He is the type of leader our state needs right now."

"Okay, Grandma, I see you've met my fiancée, Soojin," I said, butting in. "No need to lecture her on your Republican ways."

"Don't worry, Cece – regardless of who you vote for, we will continue to fight for you and the people of this state," said Soojin.

"That's if Knutson wins," Grandma continued. "I remember back in the glory years when President Reagan ran this country right. We were a shining city upon a hill back then. He was a real leader, and that Nelson reminds me of him."

Hoping to sideline the conversation, I interjected, "You're coming to our wedding, right?"

Cece started to smile. "I'll be there, my dear, don't worry," she said, patting Soojin's hand. "I was just trying to give you a hard time to see if you are cut out to be a Smith!"

I gave Soojin a playful hug, and she pushed on a pressure point in the small of my back as I said, "Thanks, Grandma; let me introduce Soojin to the rest of the family now."

Once we were out of earshot, I said, "You've never used that pressure point on me before. I think the whole left side of my body just went numb. How many pressure points do you actually know?"

"Leave me alone with Grandma Cece again and you'll find out." She smiled.

***

I proceeded to drag her from one circle of family members to the next, spinning the same story about how we met, when and where we were going to be getting married, and on and on.

After I finished the introductions, I brought her over to the rock cliffs overlooking the river where my immediate family was sitting. We watched the brave young Smiths jump down to the water below. My parents were sitting in the shade under an oak tree. All four of my siblings sat next to them – my two older brothers, Joseph Junior and Thomas, and my two younger siblings, Travis and Jill. As the middle three children, Thomas, Travis and I all knew Junior and Jill received most of our parents' attention growing up. Junior was the first-born, and Jill was Mommy's Little Princess.

Soojin and I plopped down next to them on the warm green grass, and they greeted us warmly. That is, they made a big fuss about Soojin and barely noticed me.

"Hey, Coop, thanks for finally bringing Soojin up again to hang with us," said Tommy. "We thought you were hiding her from us down in the cities!"

"I'm only hiding her until after the wedding. That way she won't get cold feet and run the other way." I smiled.

"How is your work with the Governor going?" asked my mother.

"It's going really well, thanks," Soojin said. "We are busy trying to push some new legislation through the House and Senate that will increase the salaries for teachers throughout the state. It's a bill you may be interested in, given your long career as a teacher."

"Too bad I'm not teaching now!" Mom frowned. "I suppose you will have to raise our taxes to pay for this. I was watching Fox News the other night, and there was this special about how the Democrats are just squeezing out the middle class with new taxes—"

"Okay, Mom. Let's not have a political debate during our family reunion, especially if you are going to preach Fox News propaganda to us. We already heard an earful from Grandma Cece. Dad, how is retirement life going these days?" I asked quickly changing the subject.

"Not too bad. There is always something to do. In fact, I'm busier now than while I was on the force! Speaking of, when do you plan to quit your radio gig to take up the family business?"

"It seems the rest of you have law enforcement pretty much covered. I'll just keep reporting the news."

Dad had retired after thirty hard years at the Duluth Police Department. He was a well-respected officer, and the only thing his men ever gave him a hard time about was his name, Joseph Smith. He was a devout Catholic, yet his men always teased him about the Book of Mormon, Brigham Young, and the state of Utah.

Junior was a Minnesota state trooper stationed in Duluth. Tommy worked for the Border Patrol up in Thunder Bay. Travis was a police officer in Superior. Since Travis defected to Wisconsin, he was the easiest target to pick on. Even Jill was in a Criminology Master's program at UMD.

My mother wasn't in the family business. She was a retired elementary school teacher, and a darn good one from what I heard. Then there was me, the outlier of the family. At least I didn't have to put on the same rigid uniform every day or have to worry about getting shot at. But, belonging to a law enforcement family did have its advantages, especially for a reporter. If I needed a name or license plate traced I had several brothers to choose from. I also had a wealth of potential story material.

"Have any of you guys heard about this popular new drug on the market called Brown Sugar?" I asked.

Junior and Tommy shook their heads. Travis asked, "Is that what they're calling all this new heroin in region?"

"Yes. You've heard of it?"

"Well, some of the guys down at the station were talking about it the other day," said Travis. "I guess they have busted a few addicts who had the product on them. Sounds like it comes from within Minnesota somewhere. Why do you ask?"

"Wow, look at Wisconsin coming through," I said. "How do you feel about that Minnesota?" I asked my two older brothers. Returning my attention to Travis, I added, "I heard about it earlier and was just curious."

"You cooking up a story?" asked Jill.

"I don't know yet, but I think I might know someone who could enlighten me."

"Who is that?" asked Soojin.

"I have an old friend I'd like to talk to up in Hibbing." I turned to Soojin. "What do you think about doing the Mesabi Bike Trail tomorrow? We can make Hibbing our half-way point."

"Works for me, although you might have a tough time keeping up!" Soojin was tying her hair back in a ponytail. "Now, who is ready for the Smith family decision?" she asked, just before she catapulted herself over the rock cliffs toward the water below.

I looked over to my family, whose eyes were wide. "She's a keeper," my dad said.

Chapter 3

Hibbing, MN

I had christened my bright blue, two-door Jeep Wrangler
Wellstone. It was named after Paul Wellstone, the late
Democratic senator from Minnesota. It was an impulse buy
following my hire with MPR, and as long as I had a steady
paycheck, Wellstone would stay in my garage. As Soojin and
I drove on Highway 53 north out of Duluth, she helped me
brainstorm ideas for next year's family reunion, following
my selection in the Smith family decision.

When we reached the Minnesota Discovery Center in
Chisholm, we parked Wellstone and picked up the Mesabi
Bike Trail heading southwest toward Hibbing.

"Do you remember our first date?" I asked.

"How could I forget?" Soojin pedaled her black
mountain bike past me on my left. After a few hundred yards
she slowed so we could talk. "It was the first time a guy
actually took me on a date outdoors. Every other guy I dated
tried the same lame tactic. They would take me out for drinks
and try to get me to come back to their place with some
cheesy line. No class whatsoever. Plus, your epic fall into
Lake Calhoun was pretty memorable."

After Soojin agreed to the first date, I had sent a small
canoe paddle to her office with a note that said, "Balance will
be the key to our first date. Without it, you might go home
cold and wet. Meet you at Lake Calhoun an hour before
sunset." She showed up wearing a blue "Vote for Knutson
2010" t-shirt worn thin, Nike running shorts, and sandals. I

rented two standup paddle boards for a sunset paddle around Calhoun. It was our first time trying the boards, and Soojin quickly demonstrated her superior balance skills. I was not so fortunate.

"Calhoun was a bit chilly that night," I laughed. "The cold water was worth the fall, though, because you agreed to a second date."

"I'll give you that. Dates two, three, and four were quite memorable as well. Canoeing down the Mississippi River, hiking Minnehaha Falls, and biking around Hyland Lake Park." Soojin looked reflective. "I'm just glad I found someone who loves to actually *do stuff* as much as me."

"Hey, sorry about all that political talk at the family reunion yesterday," I said. "I know it was a long day, but you were a great sport about it."

"Yes, well I'm just glad Grandma Cece approved. Not sure about all the Fox News chatter, though." She winked.

"Tell me about it. I'm like a donkey lost in a jungle full of elephants."

"I can manage the Smith family reunion once a year as long as you can put up with my dad."

"Your dad does scare me a bit," I admitted. "I feel like he has never approved of me for his special daughter."

Soojin waved her hand dismissively. "That's just his way. If it was up to him, I would marry some stuffy business tycoon or high-powered attorney. No thanks."

"I sure am glad you picked me," I said. "I think we will have a fun life together even if I never break six figures on my salary."

"I'll take experiences over things any day of the week," she replied.

"Amen to that."

***

As we neared Hibbing, Soojin broke off from me to go to a nearby Caribou Coffee for a drink. When I finished with my interview, we would meet back up for lunch. My first potential source for the story was Ricky Johnson, an old fraternity friend. He was a repeat drug offender who had been in and out of jails and rehab centers since college. Last night I had checked on Ricky's Facebook page and seen that he was working at the Sammy's Pizza in downtown Hibbing. He had a recent post about getting stuck working the whole Fourth of July weekend. He wrote that any friend who stopped by would get a free slice of pizza. I wasn't going to pass up that offer. It could be my appetizer until Soojin came for lunch.

It had been a while since I had visited Hibbing, home to such legends as Bob Dylan, Roger Maris, and Kevin McHale. I turned onto Howard Street and parked my mountain bike right in front of Sammy's Pizza. I grew up on Sammy's Pizza on First Street and First Avenue in downtown Duluth, and it contributed to my freshman fifteen. The original restaurant in Hibbing had an unbeatable lunch buffet well worth the trip. The large sign posted on the restaurant wall said *Lunch Buffet 11am – 2pm*. It was only 10:15 am, but I hoped to catch Ricky on his way into work. I assumed the workers would park and enter in the back of the building, so I left my bike and walked around to the back alley. There were no cars in the back lot, so I killed time playing Monument Valley on my iPhone while I waited.

At exactly 10:30, a rusty old white four-door Ford Taurus pulled up at the back door. I had to do a double take. Ricky looked like he had aged a good ten or fifteen years since I last saw him three years ago. Once the skinny man in our college fraternity, all that delicious Sammy's pizza had turned him into what can best be described as Zach Galifianaki's character, "Alan", in *The Hangover* movie series. Ricky even had Alan's shaggy brown hair and full beard. I assumed Sammy's work regulations required Ricky to wear both a hair and beard net to make sure no stray hair got mixed in with the cheese. He had huge dark bags under his bloodshot eyes, and his skin was pale.

I ran up to him just as he reached for the door.

"Ricky, how are you, old friend?"

Ricky spun around and looked puzzled. Then his demeanor changed, and he approached me for one of his infamous bear hugs. *Funny, just like Alan from the* Hangover *movie again.*

"Brother Coop! Can it be? Cooper the old party pooper!"

"That one never gets old. It's good to see you. You look like you've aged two decades since I last saw you. What gives?"

"Hey brother, tell me about it," Ricky said, slapping me on the shoulder.

Ricky used the word *brother* loosely with everyone he talked to.

"Hey, do you think we could chat for a few minutes before your shift starts?"

"Sure, brother, but I have to get in there soon to start warming up the ovens. But we can chat while I have a quick smoke."

Ricky grabbed a pack of Marlboro Reds out of his front breast pocket, fished a lighter out, and lit one up.

"You want one?"

"No, I'm good. So, how have you been?"

"Well, you know how it is. It's been a series of highs and lows, but mostly lows lately. I'm still on parole for getting caught with drugs again this past year. I got out of jail a few months ago and picked up this gig as a master pizza chef on a recommendation from my parole officer."

"Sounds terrible," I said, waiting to see if he would say more.

"Yeah, brother. Plus, my girlfriend just dumped me. I also got into a fight up at Palmer's Tavern. Had to spend the night in the local jail for that one. My parole officer chewed me out good, too."

"Dang, Ricky, sounds like you've been through the ringer."

"Yeah, but that's life. How are things going for you?"

I hesitated to respond because my life was pretty much the opposite of Ricky's in every way. I decided it would be better for our rapport if I downplayed things on my end a bit.

"Just trying to make ends meet," I said. This was true enough – if I didn't break a big story for MPR, my job could be through. "Do you think I could take you up on that free slice of pizza you were posting about on Facebook?"

"You bet. I have to get these ovens started first; why don't you follow me in and I'll give you the behind-the-scenes tour before the lunch crowd shuffles in."

"Sounds like a great idea, Ricky. it's never too early to eat Sammy's Pizza."

***

I followed Ricky into the back of the restaurant, feeling like a VIP getting a special look at the kitchen in the original Sammy's. One of the waitresses came in a few minutes later to get the tables ready for the day. The ovens quickly filled the kitchen with intense heat. Sure enough, Ricky was donning a hair and beard net. He wrapped a white pizza apron that appeared to have years of grease and cheese baked into it around his belly. He slid a couple of pizzas in the oven, then directed me out into the restaurant to a corner booth.

His sleeves were rolled up now, and I could see he had a new tattoo on his inner left arm that said *The Dark Side of the Moon* in cursive letters.

"Nice tattoo, when did you get that?"

He glanced at it. "I got it about a year ago. That is my favorite Pink Floyd album of all time. When you're high listening to that album, it's a trip. A real trip."

"Yeah, I can only imagine." I paused, then decided to just dive in. "So, I know you are short on time, and I want to be upfront with you. We were good buddies back in college, but I know I haven't seen you in a while. The reason I stopped by today is that I'm a reporter now for MPR down in Saint Paul. I just started working on a story, and I was hoping you could point me in the right direction. You have a lot of things going on in your life right now, and I know that. I will not be offended if you tell me to leave you be."

Ricky waved off my comments. "Don't be silly, we go way back! I'd love to help you with your story. Congrats, both on the position and the move down to the big city. I can't believe you can stand living down there, though." He leaned back in the booth. "But go ahead; ask me anything."

"It's kind of personal. Would it be better if we had this conversation at your place after your shift?"

"I'm actually busy later. Let's just chat now."

"Okay, Ricky, so I know you've had some trouble in the past with drugs. I also know you are tied-in deep with some networks—"

"Woah, are you going to use my name in this story?" Ricky looked startled.

"Don't worry, I'm not going to use your name or anything you say in my report. I just need some help here. I need you to educate me."

"All right, brother, but don't go quoting me or I'm in big trouble."

"No need to worry, this story has nothing to do with you. I just need some information to get me started."

"What do you want to know?"

"Have you heard about a new drug out on the streets called Brown Sugar?"

Ricky leaned in close to me. "Brother, how do you, of all people, know about Brown Sugar?"

Score, just what I had hoped for. "I heard someone mention it the other day and was curious."

"Listen, brother. I'll tell you what I know, but you have to make sure this doesn't get back to me."

"The last thing I want is for your safety to be in jeopardy. I'll do everything I can to protect you."

Ricky glanced over his shoulder, then lowered his voice as he talked. "Okay. So, Brown Sugar is the label for some of the purest heroin being sold on the market right now. I've heard the opium is being shipped in from Mexico. From there, the drugs make their way into Minnesota. How they get here, I'm not sure. I do know the primary supplier and top dealer in Minnesota is a guy out of Minneapolis. He goes by Smokey."

"Smokey, like a nickname?" I asked.

"Yes, I guess he looks like Smokey the Bear or something. I don't know his real name. Anyway, one of Smokey's guys came up to Hibbing a few weeks ago. He was a massive human being who went by the name Tank. I would describe him as the black version of Paul Bunyan, if you know what I mean. Except he didn't have a cute blue ox named Babe, and he is more likely to cut a man in half than a pine tree."

I nodded.

"Hard to miss that guy. He looked as huge as this restaurant. He was asking around at Palmers about local dealers who may be able sell the Brown Sugar up here. Someone mentioned my name, and I met the black Paul Bunyan himself. He was scary as hell. He could have crushed me with one punch. Anyway, I told him I was on parole now trying to lay low. He told me not to worry about the cops, and said they could be dealt with. He just wanted my network and access into the entire Iron Range area."

"What did you tell him?"

"What could I say in that situation?" Ricky frowned. "I was trapped! Of course I agreed to do it for him. These guys are no joke; you either work with them or they put you in the ground."

"Have you gone to the police?"

"Are you kidding me? Brother, that would be like signing my death wish."

"Okay, good point. Say, do you have any of the Brown Sugar on you? I'd like to see what it looks like."

"Let me go pull out those pizzas first – then I'll see about getting you that free slice, and possibly something else."

Ricky came back a few minutes later with a slice of pizza on a plate. He set it on the table, and at the same time smoothly slid me a small brown packet. I held it under the table while I read the label: Brown Sugar.

"How much are these selling for?" I asked.

"Twenty bucks a pop, brother. It's twice as expensive as the stuff we used to get, but the high from it is way better. It's still way cheaper than buying synthetic drugs like OxyContin, which can go for two or three times that price on the streets."

"Thanks for the information. You are a knowledgeable man."

"Comes with painful experience."

"Hey, can I take this one off your hands?"

"Brother, I thought you didn't use stuff like this?"

"I don't. I just want it as reference in case I need it for the story."

"Okay, brother, but you didn't get it from me."

"All right, thanks." I quickly slipped it into my pocket. Then I pulled out my wallet and handed Ricky the only bill I had – a fifty.

"What's this for?"

"The slice of pizza." I winked.

"The 'pizza' only costs twenty," he replied.

"I'm not about to ask you to make change – just keep the rest as a tip for excellent service."

He nodded, then took the bill and shoved it into his pocket. "You better eat that slice while it's still hot."

I picked up the slice of pizza and took a bite. Delicious. "Ricky, can you tell me anything else about Smokey? Do you know anything else about him?"

"I can tell you two things. One, Tank drove a brand new black Cadillac Escalade up here. It stuck out big time. It must have belonged to Smokey, though, because it had Minnesota vanity plates that spelled out *DABEAR*. You know, like 'Smokey the Bear'. Second, they hardly use phones or email. They usually just show up in person when they want something."

Just as he finished talking, the waitress called out for him to get the next round of pizzas out of the oven for the opening buffet rush. She pointed to a line forming outside the front door.

"I've got to go."

"All right, sounds good. Mind if I bring my fiancée by for lunch? I'd love to introduce her to you."

"That would be fantastic!"

***

Soojin and I enjoyed a delicious Sammy's lunch buffet together when she showed up later. I had about six pieces of pizza too many, but once you start eating Sammy's, it's difficult to stop. At the end of lunch, Ricky came back out from the kitchen to say hello.

"Ricky, I'd like to introduce you to my fiancée, Soojin Kim."

"Pleased to meet you, Ricky." Soojin extended her hand.

"The pleasure is all mine." Ricky shook her outstretched hand. "Stick around for a while, and I can share some funny Cooper Smith fraternity stories from our college days."

"That's quite all right," I said. "We need to get back on our bikes to burn off some of this pizza. Thanks so much for your time, and for the information. You were a huge help. Please, let me know if you need anything from me. Do not hesitate to call." I handed him a business card.

Ricky took the card and studied it. "Impressive." He looked back up. "Watch your back, brother. This is a dangerous world to be poking your nose into."

"Same to you, Ricky. Be safe."

As we biked out of Hibbing, I couldn't stop thinking about what Ricky had told me. Although I knew he had connections to the drug world, I hadn't expected him to be so close to the front lines of the Brown Sugar epidemic. I had a bad feeling his troubles were only just beginning.

Chapter 4

Saint Paul, MN

As Wellstone lumbered south on I-35 toward Saint Paul, I was deep in thought. My meeting with Ricky gave me a good starting point for the story. Earlier in the drive, I talked with Soojin about the conversation I had with him; even though he was out of prison, my meeting with him had saddened me. It made me nervous to think of Smokey looking over his shoulder. Ricky was clearly in a tough situation – possibly life-threatening.

As we drove in silence, I thought back to how I had grinded through job after low-paying job in local news in Duluth. After college, the only place that would hire me was *Kool 101.7*, an oldies station. That was about as far from the news as you could get in radio. In the three short months I worked there, I listened to Buddy Holly's "Peggy Sue" so many times I think I could sing it backward still today.

I then found a position with *WDIO's Eyewitness News* on the local Duluth television subscription plan. Except I wasn't working the news there, either – I was working "Eyewitness Sports," covering local high school sports. I'll never forget the time I returned to my high school, East High, to cover a varsity football game. I saw parents I still knew from when I played there years before. They smiled and greeted me warmly at the game, but I could just hear them thinking, *Wow, looks like this guy didn't make it too far from home.* I lasted only four months at *WDIO,* then I quit.

I had the pearly white teeth, but I knew I lacked the face for television, so I returned to where my true passion was – radio. I scored a position as a reporter for *KDAL* 610 AM in Duluth, a local news, weather, and sports station. This time I was there to cover the actual news. I actively went out in the community and gave the people of Duluth the news they deserved. After two years of hard work, I received a call back from an application I submitted to MPR.

I worried about my longevity at MPR, and wasn't sure what I would do if I was cut. All I knew was I didn't want to go back to making $7.50 an hour listening to Buddy Holly sing about Peggy Sue, nor did I want to cover my alma mater's football games. And as much as I loved Duluth, I wanted to chase bigger stories. I longed to chase people like Smokey. It was my calling.

"You know…" Soojin broke the silence. "If you convinced Ricky to work with you and the authorities, you may just be able to get him out of this jam."

"How so?"

"Ricky's a low-level drug dealer, but he has access to Smokey's network. I'm sure the authorities would be quite interested in this connection."

"Oh, yeah. The hard part will be to convince Ricky to come on board. He would need upfront assurances for both his safety and immunity."

"I think his cooperation is realistic, given his situation."

"Good point. First, let me call Junior and see if he can get me some more information on Smokey."

***

Junior answered my call just as we entered Saint Paul. "What's going on, Coop? Please don't tell me you're in a ditch somewhere on the interstate. Mom's making tater-tot hot dish tonight, and I plan to head straight there after my shift to eat it while it's hot."

"Hey, super trooper. Nothing like that, but I do need your help."

"What can I do you for?"

"Can you run a license plate and two nicknames for me please?"

"What am I looking for?"

"I have a tip on a potential drug dealer's license plate, and nicknames of two people affiliated with the vehicle. If you could provide me the full background story on the owner of the vehicle, and anything you can find on those nicknames, I would greatly appreciate it."

"Is this related to the Brown Sugar drug you were talking about the other day?"

"Yes, and one of my old college buddies is roped into it. I just want to know how much trouble he could actually be in."

"How much are you willing to pay for this?" asked Junior.

"Pay?"

"Yes, how much will you pay for each trace?"

"Well, I guess—"

"I'm just messing with you, baby brother. What do you have for me?"

I provided the license plate and nicknames that Ricky gave me. I was hoping Junior could figure out the vehicle's owner based on what I had. He said it was a slow Sunday at work and he promised to call me back with the results by the end of the day as long as it didn't cut into his hot dish time.

***

I kissed Soojin and dropped her off at the apartment she shared with two other women in the heart of downtown Saint Paul on Fourth Street. I lived just up the road in a one-bedroom apartment at the intersection of Selby Avenue and Dale Street, right across from the Mississippi Market Co-op.

People often asked why we didn't live together to save money. We were both raised in the church and wanted to marry first before sharing a place. Plus, I was afraid of what Soojin's father would do to me if he found out we were living together. Soojin grew up in a non-denominational Christian church, and I was an Irish Catholic. Given our slightly different religious backgrounds, we decided to get married at the James J. Hill Center in downtown Saint Paul. Soojin knew several board members for the Center, and was able to reserve it for a reasonable price for both our wedding and the reception.

I parked Wellstone and went up to my tiny, dismal apartment. It was in a musty old brick building, smelled of mold, and had serious ventilation problems. The walls were painted white, and nothing hung on them. I had a few functional pieces of IKEA furniture, including a collapsible kitchen table, two foldable chairs, a single couch, and a twin bed. My apartment was something like the intersection of how a Spartan lives and a psych ward looks.

I threw my bags down and turned on my iMac. I wanted to check my work email and get ready for the week ahead. Pending an early morning meeting and approval from my managing editor, Bill Anderson, I would be busy all week laying the groundwork for my biggest story to date.

I opened up my browser and saw that I was already logged into Facebook. I normally ignore my Facebook feed, but a posting for a planned memorial in Hibbing caught my eye. Several of my friends had commented on the story. I clicked into it.

Local Pizza Worker Found Dead in Park.

A lump rose in my throat. The article read:

A 25-year-old male named Richard Johnson from Hibbing, Minnesota was found dead this morning in Bennett Park. The victim had two gunshot wounds to the chest. Johnson was last seen at midnight in the nearby Palmer Tavern. The motives for the shooting are unclear, but authorities say he was on parole for several drug charges and may have been connected to dangerous drug networks. Johnson had been working at Sammy's Pizza as part of his parole requirements. Authorities say they will provide further details once they become available.

I felt sick to my stomach. Ricky and I had had lunch thirty hours before, and now he was dead. I rubbed my forehead as I felt a migraine coming on. My phone rang, and I jumped. It was Junior.

"Junior, something bad happened," I croaked.

"What is it?"

"Remember I told you I met an old friend yesterday in Hibbing? He was the one tied to this drug network I'm researching."

"Yeah, what happened?"

"He was found dead this morning in a park."

"That's terrible. Was it a drug overdose?"

"He was shot twice in the chest."

"Are you serious? Who shot him?"

"I don't know for sure, but I have a pretty good idea who it might be. Did you finish tracing that license plate and nicknames I gave you?"

"Yes, but I should warn you: You may be getting a visit really soon from some DEA agents."

"Wait, what?" I asked. "Why?"

"I ran the information you provided me in the National Crime Information Center database. I got a hit on Smokey's nickname and looked at his NCIC record. It must have triggered an alert with DEA, because within minutes of looking at the record they called me. Apparently he is tied to some big case DEA is working right now. They wouldn't give me details, but asked a lot of questions about why I was searching for him. They pressed me hard, Coop, and I had to tell them about you. They asked for your address and phone number and said they would be visiting you really soon. I suspect with this new Ricky development they could be there anytime."

"Holy smokes. This is a big deal. What did your trace results find?"

"Nothing on Tank, but Smokey has a long profile on NCIC. I correlated that with his photo from his driver's license tied to his vehicle. His real name is Tyrone Carter, and he's been busted twice already in Minnesota on drug charges. In 1999 he was convicted of trafficking large amounts of cocaine. In 2008, he was caught with more than three thousand OxyContin pills. Following that arrest, he was sentenced to five years in prison, but he got out on good behavior at the end of 2011."

I was typing furiously on my computer as Junior talked. My blood was pumping fast.

"That's all I have, but it should get you started. Also, a word to the wise, make sure to play ball with the DEA. If you don't, they can find ways to make your life miserable."

"Thanks, I'll pay you back with a nice steak dinner next time I'm up in Duluth."

"Deal, now it's time for hot dish. Later."

"Eat some for me. Thanks again – bye."

Just as I lifted the phone away from my ear, a loud knock sounded at my door.

I crept to the door and peeked through the eyehole. I saw two men flashing their credentials. *Wow, these guys moved fast.*

I slid the door open and asked, "How can I help you gentlemen?"

"Mr. Smith?"

"Yes?"

"My name is Agent Sosa, and this is my partner Agent Lindberg. We're with the Drug Enforcement Administration and we need a few minutes of your time to ask you some questions."

"Not a problem. Can I look at your badges and credentials first?"

"Sure," they said in unison, handing them over to me for inspection.

I had no idea what I was actually looking for, but these badges seemed legit. The names on the credentials read Special Agents Sam Sosa and Cal Lindberg.

"Any relation to the baseball player?" I asked Sosa.

"The slugger goes by Sammy. I'm just Sam." Sosa's voice sounded weary, as though he had heard that question one too many times in his life.

"Come on in. Can I get you guys something to drink?"

"Coffee is fine if you have it," said Lindberg.

"Sure. Make yourselves at home while I prepare it."

I gestured toward the couch, an IKEA special so uncomfortable you would have to go to a chiropractor if you ever accidently fell asleep on it. I luckily had some J & S Bean Factory coffee beans already grinded, and I began to prepare a fresh pot for the agents. I glanced into the living room and noticed they were both looking around my apartment. I had little for them to go on – unless my minimalism itself was a clue for the trained agents.

Sosa appeared to be of Hispanic descent. He was my height, with short dark hair, and a clean-shaven face. He wore a tight muscle shirt under a blue blazer. He clearly hit the free weights hard at the gym. He wore jeans and dress shoes, and he moved with confidence and authority. Lindberg was a tall and thin, pale, balding white man with a short, trim beard. He wore a long-sleeved button-up shirt with a black blazer, jeans, and dress shoes. He seemed to be second fiddle to Sosa.

"Any cream or sugar?" I asked.

"Black," both replied in unison.

"Have you two been partners long?"

"Why?" they both asked, looking at me.

"Well, you've been here for all of three minutes and you've spoken in perfect unison three times already."

They frowned. I came out into the living room while the coffee was brewing. The agents awkwardly squeezed together on the love-seat couch, and I sat on my Swiss exercise ball that doubled as my office chair.

"Mr. Smith–"

"Call me Cooper, please."

"Okay, Cooper," said Sosa. "We talked to your brother about what happened up in Hibbing. He told us about your meeting with an old college friend, and about your interest in Brown Sugar."

"My friend was Ricky Johnson, and he was killed last night. I just found out."

"We are sorry to hear about the loss of your friend – we found out early this morning," said Lindberg.

"I understand you are working on a story for MPR," said Sosa. "We need to know what you have so far, because we're in the midst of an ongoing investigation."

"Don't spare any details," said Lindberg.

I proceeded to tell them what little I knew about Brown Sugar and Smokey. I talked about my meeting with Ricky, and mentioned my surprise about his recent death. I said I had planned to talk to my managing editor in the morning about running with the story. The agents mostly nodded and jotted down a few notes.

"Did Mr. Johnson tell you what he was asked to do for Smokey?" asked Sosa.

"Well, he said that this Tank fellow wanted him to be a new dealer for them in the Iron Range region."

"Did Mr. Johnson say anything else?" asked Lindberg.

"Nothing significant that I remember, except he did mention this was some of the best product out on the market in terms of its purity. I guess addicts are raving over it."

The agents finished writing and looked up.

"Can you grab that coffee for us? I think it may be ready," said Sosa.

"Sure, one minute."

As I walked back to the kitchen I could hear them whispering. I assumed they were planning their next move, maybe debating whether they needed to call their supervisors. Whatever they need to do next, I hoped it didn't involve long interrogations in small concrete rooms. I brought two cups of coffee out for them, and they both had to set down their notebooks because I had no coffee table for them to place their cups on.

"Cooper, we know you are working on a story," said Sosa, "but we cannot let you run that story right now, or anytime soon."

"I'm just getting started on it, so I still need some time." I paused. "But as you know, this could be a big story, so I can't wait forever."

Sosa leaned toward me. "You see, we have an active investigation against Smokey and many more individuals tied to him. If you run the story too soon, everyone, including

Smokey, will go underground. They will get away, and we will have to start from scratch," said Sosa.

"How much time do you need?" I asked.

"Four months," said Sosa.

Four months would put me in November. By then I would already be married, working with Soojin in my free time on the Governor's re-election campaign, and getting ready to leave for Europe. Soojin and I had agreed to postpone our honeymoon until November, after the busy election season had finished. I might not even have a job four months from now without a story like this under my belt.

"I don't know how long this story will take to produce, but I know I'll need a shorter timeline. I'm getting married on Labor Day weekend, and this story needs to run by then. That's seven weeks from now. Would that work for you?"

"Mr. Smith," said Sosa sternly, reverting back to addressing me formally, "Congratulations and all of that on your upcoming wedding, but this is serious. If you run the story too early, these drug suppliers and dealers will get away, and more innocent people will become addicts. Or worse, there will be more victims like your friend, Mr. Johnson."

I flinched. "You don't have to throw my friend's death in my face. I will talk to my editor tomorrow, and he will likely want me to run with the story right away. He won't care about your timeline."

"Okay, how about this," said Sosa. "We agree to work with you and share things on the case when we can, if you agree to be flexible on running your story. You can run it one minute after we take these guys down. You'll be the first one with the inside scoop."

I thought about something Junior mentioned earlier. These agents could probably put me in a really bad situation. Sosa was right about something though. In the news world, if you ain't first, you're last, just like Will Ferrell's character

Ricky Bobby said in *Talladega Nights*. If these agents were genuine in their offer to share information, I could come out ahead in the deal and still be the first with the story. I decided to play ball.

"All right, Agents Sosa and Lindberg. Just give me a few days to talk to my editor and attend Ricky's funeral. Then, I'll get back to you."

"Great, Cooper. Take as much time as you need. We look forward to working with you," said Sosa. "Can you give us some of your contact information so we can be in touch?"

"Absolutely. Let me give you my business card."

I reached into my pocket to fish out my wallet. In the process, the packet of Brown Sugar spilled out onto the floor. I froze.

"What is that?" demanded Lindberg.

"Mr. Smith, what is that?" repeated Sosa, pointing at the packet.

You have got to be kidding me. I didn't know what to say, so I told the truth about how Ricky gave it to me so I could use it for the story. They had all the leverage on me now. *Way to blow it, Cooper Smith.* Lindberg scooped it off the ground.

"That's Brown Sugar," Lindberg said, handing it to Sosa.

"Well, well, well. Looks like you are taking investigative journalism to a whole new level," said Sosa, tucking the packet into his inside blazer pocket.

I nodded in embarrassment, but was glad they weren't arresting me for it. Yet.

"You will share any new developments on this story with me personally," said Sosa, handing me his card after I passed him mine. "Do we have an understanding?"

"Yes, Agent Sosa. We have an understanding."

"Good. Let's go, Agent Lindberg. Our meeting here is done."

They both set their coffee mugs on the kitchen table on their way to the door. Lindberg went out into the hallway. Sosa stopped in the doorway and looked back at me. He pulled the Brown Sugar packet out of his pocket and waved it at me with a smile.

"Remember, if you find anything at all I want the details right away," he said.

I just stood there dumbfounded, then decided to salute Sosa in agreement. His smile turned into a slight head nod, and with that he slid into the hallway and slammed the door behind him. I was afraid my chance at my first major story had just slammed shut with it.

Chapter 5

Chicago, IL

Chicago's South Side was often referred to as Chi-raq, said to be as treacherous as war-torn Iraq. On a hot, humid, Sunday night, Tank and Smokey drove into the South Side's Englewood community, arguably one of the most dangerous communities in Chicago, if not the entire United States. Tank was driving a used Ford Explorer, instead of Smokey's Cadillac Escalade. Where they were headed, an Escalade would be a prime target.

Smokey watched for the Salvation Army on Sixty-Ninth Street. When they spotted it, Tank turned right and headed south on Green Street. After another 200 meters, Tank turned right again so they were directly behind the Salvation Army. Then, Tank took an immediate left down the alley and counted off five buildings. The safe house was the fifth building on their left. They pulled into a wooded area off the alley behind the garage, and waited.

"Has he sent the message yet?" asked Tank.

Smokey checked his phone. Sure enough, he had a message asking him to flash his front lights twice and turn off the engine.

"Flash the lights twice and kill the engine," Smokey said.

Tank did as instructed, and a few seconds later, two short, stalky men came out of the garage toward the Explorer, one on each side. Smokey and Tank got out of the vehicle and spread their arms and legs. They had been told to leave all of their weapons in the vehicle, and they obliged. The two men, who Smokey could now see were Latinos, searched them over thoroughly for weapons and wires. Once finished, they all walked toward an old, beat-up garage, not saying a word.

Inside, the garage was empty except for a metal detector in the middle of the floor with two collapsible chairs on either side of it. Smokey could now see the Latinos had full-sleeve tattoos on both arms. They wore baggy black t-shirts and blue jeans.

They motioned for Smokey and Tank to go through the metal detector. Before doing so, Tank slowly pulled out a knife that was concealed inside his boot. He threw it down on the floor. Once they were successfully through the metal detector they were led to the back of the safe house. It was a two-story brick building forty years past its prime. They followed the Latinos up the stairs to a second-floor bedroom in the middle of the house. The person Smokey had come to meet sat smoking a cigar behind a desk in a barren room.

"Hello, Captain. It's nice to finally meet you in person," said Smokey.

"Smokey, please, sit down." Captain motioned to the two chairs in front of his desk.

Smokey eyed the man known simply as Captain. His nickname came from the rank he held in the Mexican Army before joining up with the drug trade and moving to Chicago. People said he was in deep with the Los Zetas Cartel, but Smokey wasn't in a position to confirm this. Captain had an American mother, so the Cartel sent him north as their most trusted man in the Midwest. He was in his mid-fifties and had dark, leathery skin. His oversized forehead and nose, contrasted with his small, beady eyes. He had tattoos of guns up his neck and down his arms. He wore a white wife-beater tank top and sat relaxed behind his desk as he continued to suck down his cigar.

Smokey had struck up a friendship with a man named Rodriguez, one of Captain's close, trusted men, while they were both serving time in the Stillwater prison in Minnesota. Rodriguez was still doing hard time for a first-degree murder he committed in Minneapolis a few years ago. Word on the street was that Rodriguez had taken out one of Captain's primary dealers in Minnesota when he was found to be disloyal. Smokey vowed not to make the same mistake.

"I've heard a lot about you from Rodriguez," said Smokey. "He said you take care of those who work with and for you."

"Which means he told you what I do to those who cross me, right?" Captain pulled a large, bowie knife out of a drawer and set it on the table between him and Smokey. "Of course, I know I won't have that problem with you. Rodriguez vouched for you, and I trust him. He has sound judgment, and this knife here is real sharp."

"Thanks, Captain. I know you are a busy and important man, so I will keep this brief. We drove down from Minneapolis because we need more supply. The product you've sold to us is so good that demand has skyrocketed. I'd like to triple my monthly order, if possible."

Captain slowly looked Smokey up and down. "I'm pleased by this. As you know, we take on a lot of risks smuggling our product up here from Mexico, and at times the supply can be depleted. Lucky for you, we should be getting a new shipment sometime in the next week. If all goes as planned instead of the usual one-kilo per month, we can offer you three kilos. There will be more where that comes from in the future, but start with three per month and keep me posted on your progress. Are you still primarily selling to those Indians up on the reservations?"

"They are our main customers right now, but we are trying to branch into other parts of the state, and possibly into North Dakota as well," said Smokey.

"Good. Once the shipment arrives I'll have one of my men meet your guy mid-way in Wisconsin. I'll email you the specific pick-up location closer to the date," said Captain.

"Perfect. Thanks, Captain. Now, we'll head out to make us all some more money."

"Keep this up, and we will all be extremely wealthy and healthy men. Mess up, and you'll be crying like a little girl wishing you were dead. That goes for the big gorilla there, too." Captain pointed his knife at Tank. "We will have fun cutting him up piece by piece."

Tank flexed his muscles but Smokey put his hand on Tank's massive forearm.

"Just keep the shipments coming, and we will move the product," said Smokey. "Thank you for your time. We will wait for word on the new shipment."

Captain didn't respond, just took a puff of his cigar and nodded toward the door. Smokey pulled Tank up and away from the desk, and the two strode out of the room without looking back. Tank grabbed his knife from the floor of the garage on his way out, and they jumped in the Explorer and took off.

Smokey and Tank normally put the fear of God into other people, but they knew what a serious Mexican cartel could do to you if you ended up on its black list. Smokey didn't want to venture down that road. Both men held their breaths and watched the rear-view mirrors until they reached the city limits and hit I-90 West. From there, it was interstate all the way back to Minnesota.

Chapter 6

Saint Paul, MN

My alarm clock showed 6:21 am on Monday morning. *Two lousy hours of sleep, what a great start to the week.* I had tossed and turned all night thinking about everything that had transpired over the long holiday weekend. The family reunion seemed like a blur after the meeting with Ricky, and then the discovery of his death last night. Of course, the meeting with the DEA was the cherry on top that sent my head into the ultimate tailspin.

I decided a brisk morning walk would help clear my mind and wake me up. The main MPR office is located in downtown Saint Paul on Cedar Street. It is less than two miles from my apartment, and it took exactly thirty-one minutes to walk there.

I set out on foot, heading east on Selby Avenue and thinking about my upcoming meeting with Bill Anderson. Wild Bill, as we called him, was known for flying off the handle unexpectedly. *Although, was it really unexpected if it happened every meeting?* I wondered. I decided I was going to give him all of the facts and press hard to run with the story. I was a junior employee and I knew it, but this was my story. It was time for me to prove I could do more than funny interviews at the Minnesota State Fair or behind-the-scenes stories at a Vikings game. This was the news story I was born to chase. And getting it would mean I could also bring down the thugs who killed Ricky.

I turned right onto Wabasha Street, then took a left at West Exchange Street. I passed in front of the historic Fitzgerald Theater, MPR's largest broadcast studio, named after Minnesota native F. Scott Fitzgerald. One more block, and I turned right onto Cedar Street. And there it was – the MPR headquarters in all its glory. Our flagship office had two main parts – an old brick structure on the south side connected to the modern, shiny glass-windowed north side. The north side was home to what we called the UBS Forum, a large broadcast auditorium used to host community discussion, public debates, and live program recordings.

Bringing it all together was the LED-lit scrolling headline ticker that ran across the length of the old building until it attached to the entrance door on the new building. The ticker was similar to the ones seen in Times Square in New York. It was part of my morning tradition to look at the first headline on the ticker. It turned something on in my brain, and after reading it I was ready to go for the day.

Monday, July 7, 2014 –
Washington State Prepares to
Allow Sales of Recreational
Marijuana Beginning Today...

Slow news day, I thought, making my way through the lobby and up the stairs to the third floor, home to the MPR newsroom. It was one giant cubicle farm spread out across an open room. With the downsizing the newspaper industry had faced in the past few years, MPR now had one of the largest newsrooms in the Midwest. The desks had low wall partitions so you could see and yell across the room to your fellow reporter or producer. We called it the gopher pit, because people would occasionally pop their heads up and call out a breaking news story. Of course, the veterans had offices lined along the walls, which gave us worker bees something to strive for. But all the bosses were yes-men now. The real magic happened in the bullpen.

I worked in the general assignment reporting section, but longed to work with the secretive and selective investigative reporting team. They sat in a different section on the other side of the third floor. The team was comprised of one senior editor and four investigative reporters. They were known to book one of our conference rooms for months at a time, covering the windows with paper so no one could see what they were working on.

The investigative team's most recent project focused on the Catholic Church in Minnesota and was produced after months of groundwork. The series highlighted the scandals facing the Church, including corruption and the molestation of minors. As a former altar boy, I had never talked with anyone about how uncomfortable I felt when the priest rubbed my back when talking to me or touched my knee if I sat down next to him, because I thought anyone I told would say I was overreacting. He was like God to us.

I shared a cubicle with Lisa Larson, my self-proclaimed archrival. She also worked on general assignments, but she had been called upon to help the investigative team on the Catholic Church project. She must have made an impression, because I had heard rumors she was being considered for a permanent spot on the team. Since openings on the investigative team were hard to come by, I needed to make my mark soon if I wanted to pursue that position myself. I knew I would be competing with Lisa not only for the investigative team, but also for longevity with the organization.

She was from Green Bay, which was the first major strike against her. My lifelong support of the Vikings prevented me from being too fond of anyone from Packers' territory. We had started just weeks apart in 2013, and fought tooth-and-nail to win stories from each other. We were collegial to a certain extent, but when it came to a good story, we pulled no punches.

The newsroom was quiet at this early hour, and I was surprised to see Lisa was already at her desk checking email. She was in her mid-twenties, tall and thin with wavy brown hair. She dressed fashionably, wearing the latest boutique store collections with her signature blazing red glasses. The frames were so bright they could burn a hole through your eyes if you looked at them for too long.

I sat down at my desk next to her and said, "How was your Fourth of July weekend, Lisa?"

"Just like any other long holiday weekend," she replied, not looking my way.

She was starting to prove my theory that the only two good things that come out of Wisconsin were Leinenkugel beer and cheddar cheese.

"Do anything fun?" I asked.

"I went home and saw my family."

I waited a second to see if she would expound, but she was still focused on her email.

"Working on any new stories?"

"I have some things in the works," Lisa said, still not looking up. "You?"

I thought about how to answer. As much as I longed to share some details from my story, I decided to hold my tongue until I met with Bill.

"We'll see," I said.

***

Bill arrived later than normal at 9:37 am. I had already been at work for two hours and my patience was running thin. I decided to gamble and approach him on his way into his office. I knew once he was logged in he would be catching up on emails and reading through headlines. I casually caught up with him while he was a few feet from his office.

Bill was in his mid-forties, tall with a pudgy frame caused by years of sedentary lifestyle choices. He was bald with an eternal five o'clock shadow. He had intense eyes and his nose bent to one side. He wore his usual tight sweater vest, which highlighted his beer belly. He didn't care.

"Good morning, Bill. I hope you had a nice weekend."

"Is that right, Cooper? Why is this morning a particularly good morning?"

"Well, that's what I was hoping to talk to you about. I think I'm on the cusp of breaking a major story for us."

"What makes you think that?" Bill set his bag down and turned on his computer.

"Because two federal agents from the DEA came to my house last night and told me I couldn't report on it yet."

That got Bill's attention. He looked up at me with curiosity in his eyes. I proceeded to tell him everything I knew about Brown Sugar, Ricky, and Smokey and his guys. I talked about the drug problem on the reservations in northern Minnesota. When I finished, Bill stopped to take a few notes.

He's interested, but tell him everything first. It's the only way.

"This is a good morning indeed, Cooper. Although I'm sorry to hear that your friend died." Bill paused. "Anyway, I don't care what those agents told you last night; we have the constitution supporting our right to run our story as soon as we deem it ready. So what's your plan – how are you going to stay ahead of this?"

"Well, there's a slight problem."

"What kind of problem?"

"When I was passing my business card to the agents last night, a packet of Brown Sugar I acquired from Ricky slipped out of my pocket. They spotted it and in not so many words said they wouldn't cause any legal problems for me if I played ball with them. Meaning I had to wait until they took the drug ring down before we could run the story."

Here it comes, get ready. I looked down and held my breath.

Bill balled his right fist and pounded it into the table. I could feel everyone's eyes in the newsroom on the back of my head as they turned to see one of Wild Bill's infamous freak-outs.

"You have got to be kidding me! In what world did you think it was okay to take drugs, heroin no less, and be stupid enough to drop it in front of two DEA agents? Were you even thinking? Perhaps you thought you were still up north working for your local college radio. I bet you did drugs in the studio all the time up there!"

Local college radio comment, that was a low blow Wild Bill.

There wasn't much I could say or even respond to. Once Bill was on a roll, it was best to look down like a defeated puppy being scolded. Bill's face was red. Then he said something right out of my worst of nightmares.

"Maybe I should put Larson on it. I know she at least has the sensibility to refrain from buying drugs, and she's from Wisconsin for crying out loud. Do you know the types of things those people are into over there?"

"Bill, if I may—"

"They tip cows over at night like it's some sort of game."

Bill started to pace. "Listen, Cooper. I'll give you one chance to stay on this story, but you better think of something good, and you better think of it soon."

I had spent all night tossing in my bed thinking about how to respond to this very scenario. I knew Bill liked to put pressure on, and I was ready for it.

"I think I can get a source inside the reservation through a connection I have in Bemidji. I can try to work the network from the bottom up while the DEA works it from the top down. If I share what I find with the DEA, I think they'll play ball on their end."

"Who is your connection?"

"I'm sorry, but I can't tell you that – for his protection."

I planned to call Jesse, given his work in Bemidji near the reservation. I hoped Jesse could help me find a source – someone he had leverage on who could report on the drug network on the reservation.

"Coop, what's your goal here?"

"My goal with this story would be to highlight the drug epidemic in the state, and help authorities bring down Smokey and his network."

Bill steepled his fingers. "I'm not talking just about this story – what is your goal here at MPR?"

"I'd love to join the investigative team one day, and work on longer-term, high impact projects."

"It's good to have ambitions, and the investigative team is a nice goal to strive for." He glanced over my shoulder at the door, then lowered his voice. "I probably don't need to remind you of our 'Last-In-First-Out' policy. I'm not saying we will have job cuts for sure, but if we do, they'll be looking at the few of you who were most recently hired. You would be included in the 'Last-in' part of the equation, so I'm sure you can understand what the rest would mean for you. Now, you need to approach this story with everything you have. Use the death of your friend as a motivation to get back at these thugs. Remember that shining a light on this issue will help prevent others from making the same mistakes your friend did. I need your full effort here."

"I'll chase this story with everything I have." I stood. "Speaking of Ricky, can I take Wednesday off to go up to his funeral? I'll start on the story full bore when I return."

Bill eyed me up and down. "Okay, Cooper. Run with your story after your friend's funeral – I'll get you a budget and resources. But keep me posted, and don't let it get away from you. I don't want to follow any other news outlets on this one. And, remember, the story will need breadth and depth. Anyone can identify a bunch of drug dealers and addicts, but I need you to go out and tell their stories. There are a dozen or more rehab centers in the Twin Cities area. Go interview some of the addicts affected by heroin. Also, try to get me an interview if you can secure a source up on the reservation. We can mask his voice for protection, but it would add significantly to the story. It would also show me you are ready for the big leagues."

"Thanks, Bill. I'm going to be so far ahead on this story we will have everyone chasing us, including the *Star Tribune, Pioneer Press, Kare11, Fox9*, and maybe even some national media outlets."

I knew that would satisfy Bill – he still held a grudge against the *Star Tribune* for firing him when the newspaper industry went belly up.

"Let's hope that is the case, young man. I love it when all those competitors are mouth breathing outside on Cedar Street watching our headline ticker float by." Bill gazed out his window to the street below. "You can't beat that. It's what gets me up in the morning."

I thought his ulcer-inducing tantrums got him up in the morning – but I would have to make a mental note of this Wild Bill tidbit.

"Just don't screw it up." He turned back around to face me. "Or I'll send you back up north to whatever Podunk town you called home. You'll be covering local high school sports for the rest of your career."

I began to back out of his office. As I left, Bill got in one last jab.

"And you won't even be covering varsity football – you'll be on the JV volleyball circuit. Think about that, Cooper. Think about that."

I thought about it, all right. I thought about it a lot. Time to get my story.

Chapter 7

Wisconsin Dells, WI

Smokey and Captain agreed to have their men meet in the Wisconsin Dells, roughly halfway between Minneapolis and Chicago, for the exchange. All the tourist attractions provided plenty of cover for the men to hide in the noise.

Smokey sent Jimmy, his most trusted man. This was Smokey's biggest purchase yet, and he did not want it getting screwed up. Jimmy chewed on a toothpick as he headed southeast down I-90. After three hours of driving he found his exit, number 87. He gnawed his toothpick so hard that it snapped – the third one in the past thirty minutes. He knew there was a lot riding on this, and he was a little nervous. He turned off the interstate and headed east on Highway 13, following the road until he saw a gigantic sign featuring Paul Bunyan and Babe the Blue Ox.

Paul Bunyan's Cook Shanty offered all-you-could-eat breakfast, lunch, and dinner starting at 7 am and running until 8 pm closing time. Jimmy watched the final ray of sun fall past the horizon and looked at his Cadillac's clock – 8:39 pm. The meeting was scheduled for 9, and Jimmy wanted to be a few minutes early so he could scope out the area.

As he pulled into the parking lot, Jimmy noticed the restaurant was pitch black, with no cars parked in front. He headed around back to the far corner of the overflow parking lot, which was invisible from the main road and also empty. It was the perfect cover for a clandestine exchange. Jimmy parked his vehicle, killed the engine and lights. He grabbed a fresh toothpick, and waited.

***

The parking lot was surrounded on three sides with thick trees, which provided Agents Sosa and Lindberg with excellent cover. They waited in their unmarked Ford Crown Victoria in the woods directly north of the overflow parking lot. They had a decent view of the parking lot on the side of the tree line so they could shoot pictures of the exchange. Sosa also had agents positioned in the trees on the other two sides of the parking lot. They were on standby waiting for Sosa's signal.

Sosa had been monitoring Smokey's email address following approval from the surveillance courts. Captain was known to email meeting details to his dealers at the last moment in case one of them was working with the authorities. The short window of time would make it difficult for law enforcement to stage an ambush. Today was no exception. Sosa had intercepted an email message between Smokey and Captain that afternoon with the specifics. He and Lindberg high-tailed it from the Minneapolis field office down to the Dells to set up before the exchange. They arrived at 7:58 pm as the restaurant was closing down for the night. It was now 8:41, they saw a vehicle's lights come into the parking lot from the main road. When the vehicle turned into the back overflow parking, Sosa could see it was a black Cadillac CTS with Minnesota plates.

At 9:01 pm, a brand new silver Mercedes S-Class Sedan with Illinois license plates arrived and crept toward the Cadillac. Lindberg was busy clicking away with his Canon DSLR camera with a night vision adapter connected to a long-range telephoto lens. It was top-of-the-line equipment that would capture nighttime exchanges with enough clarity to be used as evidence in court.

"Are you getting this, Lindberg?" asked Sosa.

"Yes, I've got both vehicles and plates. There's Mr. Toothpick, and now Mr. Mute," said Lindberg, using the code names for Jimmy and the Latino.

"Keep clicking and get ready for the exchange."

***

The Mercedes parked next to Jimmy's Cadillac, and both men got out of their vehicles. Jimmy chewed his shredded toothpick, while the Latino threw out a recently finished cigarette. Smokey had told Jimmy the Latino never spoke a word, so it was better to just get down to business.

Jimmy grabbed his small duffel bag and handed $150,000 cash in $10,000 stacks over to the Latino. The Latino looked it over and did a quick count. Once he was satisfied, he went around to his trunk and popped it open. On the side of the trunk was a secret compartment. The Latino grabbed three bags, each containing one kilo of heroin. He handed them over to Jimmy, who quickly put them in his duffel. Jimmy nodded to the Latino, and they both headed back to their cars. The Latino jumped in his Mercedes and pulled out of the parking lot.

Jimmy was told to wait a few minutes to make sure the Latino was clear before he departed. He took the time to start on a new toothpick and inspect the product in his bag, just to be sure.

***

Sosa knew the window between the exchange and the time Jimmy would depart was small. The message he intercepted said that Jimmy was to wait a few minutes before departing to ensure Captain's man was gone.

"All agents on standby," said Sosa over the radio as soon as Mute left the area. "Once Mute is out on the main road past the tree line, we make our move."

"We're clear," said an agent on surveillance at the Burger King just west of their position.

"Move, now!" called Sosa on the radio.

All four agents on either side of the woods descended on Toothpick on foot while Sosa drove his sedan up behind Toothpick's Cadillac. As the agents reached Toothpick's vehicle, they could see he was looking down into his lap.

***

Jimmy finished looking over the last bag of product. Everything was there. The boss was going to be happy for sure.

All of a sudden, he saw movement in the shadows out of the corner of his eye. Before he could reach for his gun, four men dressed in black surrounded him, assault rifles at the ready. *What the hell?* Jimmy nearly choked on his toothpick as he slapped his hands up on the dash. He wasn't prepared to die tonight.

A police cruiser directly behind his car blocked his escape. A brawny Hispanic man walked briskly up to Jimmy, instructing him to get out of the car slowly. *This cannot be happening.* Jimmy obliged and was immediately taken down to the pavement. His face was shoved into the gravel as a knee drove into his upper back. They handcuffed him.

"I'm Agent Sosa with the DEA," the Hispanic man said. "You're coming with me."

***

We got you buddy – now the DEA owns you. Sosa's adrenaline was sky high as he dragged Toothpick up on his feet and threw him in the back of his vehicle. They had a mobile interrogation trailer on its way up from the Chicago field office. They planned to have a really good chat with Toothpick tonight.

Once the trailer arrived, they parked it behind the trees by the police cruiser. They wanted to keep the meeting with Toothpick discreet, because they had no plans to bring him in. Instead, they would use him against his boss.

***

How did this go wrong? I followed the instructions perfectly. Jimmy knew he couldn't go to jail; he heard too many horror stories from Smokey.

The agents dragged Jimmy into an RV-like trailer. *Unreal.* Smokey was literally going to kill him, if he made it out of this at all. Then he thought about the timing, and realized the DEA had already been in place before he arrived. *It was a set up. Was it the Latino? Or was it Captain?* His mind raced as Sosa sat down across from him in a tiny room barely big enough for the two of them.

"Mr. James Jones, you are in big trouble my friend," said Sosa. "What is Smokey going to think when he finds out about this? I suspect you'll be done for."

Thanks for stating the obvious, you arrogant prick. Jimmy didn't say a word, just stared at the floor, thinking about his options. *I could run for it. No, that's dumb, I would never get away. I could lie, but that's no use, either. They had him dead to rights.*

"Oh, I'm sorry. You go by Jimmy, right? Well, hello, Jimmy. It's so nice to finally meet you. As I mentioned, my name is Agent Sosa. Now, we found three kilos of heroin in your bag. That's some serious stuff; we could put you away for a long time with that amount. And by put you away, I mean prison. Prison, being the same thing as execution, because we both know Smokey would make sure you were a dead man in prison. Isn't that right?"

Jimmy was pissed now, and he didn't even have a toothpick to chew on. *If only he could waste this guy and get out of here.*

"But, don't worry, Jimmy. I know you're not cut out for prison, and I'd hate to see you get shanked in the shower, or worse... So, I have a deal for you. Right now, no one except us knows about this meeting. Smokey doesn't know, Captain doesn't know, no one knows. We could let you walk out of here tonight like nothing ever happened."

"In return for what?"

"The man speaks!" said Sosa. "For a minute there, I thought you were like that Latino mute who can't even muster a single word."

"What do you want me to do?" Jimmy raised his voice.

"Easy, tough guy. I hold all the cards here, so listen up. We want to take down everyone. That means Smokey, his whole crew, Captain and his men, and your primary dealers up in Red Lake and White Earth. We want the whole network from Chicago to Bemidji."

Is this guy serious? Jimmy wondered. *I would be a dead man walking if I took down Smokey's network. It would take them all of two minutes to know it was me that crossed them.*

"Jimmy, I know what you're thinking. Dead if I do, dead if I don't. But fear not, for Uncle Sam has your back. In return for your full cooperation, and the successful takedown of the whole drug ring, we are willing to offer you full amnesty, plus relocation with a whole new identity. We will even throw in some protection initially, until you can get settled."

"What happens when they find out and order a hit on me from prison?" asked Jimmy.

"Well, this is where your superior acting skills come into play. We will take you down with the rest of them. You will go to prison, and then we will have you transferred. The transfer won't be to Stillwater; it'll be to a new life in a state far away."

"Let me guess, Alaska?"

"Wow, you're a tough guy, and you're funny. We'll try to find you a nice home in the lower forty-eight, but keep in mind there is no state income or sales tax in Alaska. Something to think about as you plan for your future."

He considered. "What do you need me to do?"

"Now we're talking. We've got Smokey's connection to Captain on camera thanks to your exchange tonight. What we don't have are Smokey's dealers on the reservations. We're going to need you to wear a wire and get Smokey on tape admitting to his drug network up on the reservations. I'm talking names, dollar amounts, and times. We use the recording as evidence on Smokey, and then we take down the dealers the next time you sell them the product."

"If one of those guys gets arrested, Smokey will know and go into hiding," said Jimmy.

"That's precisely why we need a trusted man like you to convince Smokey to send two guys out at the same time to deliver the goods. Tell him it's safer to split the product so it's not all with one person. Speaking of, has he told you how he plans to distribute it?"

Jimmy hesitated, but he knew he was all the way in now. "Yeah, he wants to send a kilo to each reservation, and use the other kilo to enter new markets in Minnesota."

"Markets like the Iron Range?"

"Yes, and reservations in North Dakota, too."

"Jimmy, did you kill Mr. Johnson up in Hibbing last weekend?"

Whoa, what? Jimmy was thrown off. A few days ago he had heard Tank telling Smokey about how he had to waste one of their drug dealers in Hibbing, but he only listened passively and couldn't remember everything.

"I don't have many details, but I heard one of my colleagues, Tank, blasted a dealer up there."

Sosa looked at him and started to laugh. "That's what they all say, Jimmy. It was the other guy, not me. You know, our deal might change if we found out you killed in cold blood."

"Listen, I didn't kill that guy. Smokey always sends Tank to do that kind of work. I overheard Tank tell Smokey he thought the dealer in Hibbing had shorted him. When Tank searched the guy's wallet he found a business card for some reporter. When pressed, the dealer admitted to talking to him. Tank blasted the guy, took the card, and gave it to Smokey. That's all I heard."

"I believe you. Remember, we are friends. I know you aren't a murderer like the rest of those guys. Now, it's extremely important for me to know when Smokey sends that product up to the reservations. We need to take everyone down at once. I have this non-traceable phone for you here. The only phone number programmed on it is mine. My phone is attached to my hip 24/7, and I want you to send me a message once you have the confirmed names, dates, and locations for the exchanges between your men and the dealers on the reservations. Also, here is the wire. It's got a microphone and a recording element. It's not big and bulky like in the movies, so you should be able to conceal it easily with your baggy clothes. Wear it when you give Smokey the goods, and get the information that links him to the reservations. It's as easy as that, my friend. Once you've done your part, we'll do ours. Just don't go running away on me. You know we'll find you, and things won't go well for you then."

"All right. Just keep me safe. My life is on the line here."

"Safety's my middle name," said Sosa. "They call me Sam 'the Safety Man' Sosa up in the office. You follow my instructions, and you'll have nothing to worry about."

"Okay, man. Just don't hang me out to dry."

"I won't. Now, go get me Smokey and his network."

Chapter 8

Saint Paul, MN

I-94 heading west out of Saint Paul might as well have been a parking lot. There was a twelve-car pileup that morning, and I had an important meeting to get to. I was able to pull together a group of five recovering heroin addicts for an interview at the rehabilitation center in Plymouth. I was not about to reschedule on these people. They were going through a lot, and I knew I was a distraction to their program.

To make the traffic jam productive, I called Jesse. *Please have a source for my story, please.* If not, Wild Bill would give my story to Lisa. My Bluetooth synced with the vehicle's audio and Jesse answered on the third ring.

"Hey, Coop, what's going on?"

"How is my favorite cousin doing today?"

"Not bad, the fish have been biting really good this week down on Lake Irving."

"Good to hear. Say, I need a huge favor from you."

"How huge?"

"Remember last weekend when you were telling me about the big drug problem up there on the reservations?"

"Yeah?"

"Well, I know it's wishful thinking, but I was wondering if you might have any sources connected to the main dealer there on Red Lake. If not, I would even take someone sitting in your jail right now with the right connections."

"What would you need from them?"

"I need someone willing to be recorded who can identify the main drug dealer and network there in Red Lake. I would, of course, mask the person's voice for protection. No identifying questions will be asked, but I need someone who is in the know."

"I can tell you we don't have the time or resources to run sources, so I can't help you there. But just this past week we picked up someone who falls directly below the main dealer on Red Lake in the Brown Sugar pyramid scheme. He got out on bail, but it wouldn't take much to get him back to see if he would talk. I know he was pretty scared when he was here, so he might play ball."

"Jesse, that would be awesome. Did your guy say who the main dealer is?"

"Yes, a local native named Jason Red Eagle. He's the point person who works with the supplier out of Minneapolis. The guy we brought in, his name is Roy Cloud. You'd have to come up here in person though, because he won't do this kind of thing over the phone."

"Wow, thanks. Of course I would come up there. Just let me know when you think you can setup a meeting with Cloud and I'll make arrangements to swing up."

"Sounds good, Coop, just don't–"

I looked down at my phone and saw Agent Sosa was calling. "Hey, I hate to cut you off, Jesse, but I'm getting another call I need to take."

"I was going to say don't get your hopes up, but I'll see what I can do. Later."

"Bye."

I switched to the other call. "Agent Sosa, how are you doing?"

"I'm doing fine, Cooper. Listen, I need to talk to you about something very important."

"What is it?"

"We have some new information that suggests you have been placed on a list."

"What kind of list?"

"The kind of list you don't want to be on. Do you remember your meeting with Mr. Johnson last weekend?"

"Yes, of course. I just got back from his funeral late last night."

"Well, Tank found your business card in Ricky's wallet, and Smokey's watching you now. We don't believe it's an actual hit list at this point, but if you pursue this story you could be in danger."

Wellstone continued to idle in the standstill traffic. I was sick to my stomach. I thought about opening the door and throwing up the Honey Nut Cheerios I'd had for breakfast.

"Cooper, are you there?"

"Yes, I just. I just need a minute."

"I know this may be a lot to take in, but the important thing is you should be fine as long as you get off the story."

"What if I take a more passive role and don't push too hard?" I asked. As sick as I felt, I was not throwing this story away.

"Hey, tough guy, I don't know if you heard me. Do you remember what happened to your buddy up in Hibbing? Do you want to join him?"

"I have to think about it."

"You'll have to do better than that. In fact, I don't want your death on my hands, so if you don't agree to stop I'm going to have to pay a visit to your office and make sure your boss takes you off."

And that would be the ballgame for me. The second Sosa stepped into Bill's office, I would be off the story. And as soon as Sosa stepped out of the building, Lisa Larson would be on it. I decided to gamble and push back.

"If Ricky was really killed as a result of my interaction with him, there is no way I'm going to sit on the sidelines while his killers run free. What's more, I have a potential source inside Red Lake who is connected to the new boss, Jason Red Eagle."

"What's his name?"

"You know I can't tell you that. But I'm willing to share any pertinent information I obtain from him… if you agree not to go to my boss."

Sosa paused. "Aren't you afraid of Smokey?"

"Yes, I clearly know the risks. The dirt is still fresh on Ricky's coffin."

"We can help line up a meeting."

"I'll keep that in mind. Do you have any updates you can share with me?"

"We have some positive developments in the works, but I can't go into any details with you. The main thing for you to worry about is avoiding Smokey and his crew. I want a full readout if you are able to interview your source. Please obtain as much information as you can about Jason Red Eagle."

"Sounds good. Best of luck to you on your investigation. I hope we can get all of these guys behind bars soon."

Traffic started inching forward.

"We will, Cooper. Soon enough."

With that, we both hung up. If I could make it over to Highway 169 North in the next ten minutes, I could still make my appointment.

***

My phone rang again; this time it was Soojin. I was glad she called; I wanted to fill her in on my conversations with Jesse and Sosa.

"Hey, babe, how are you doing?"

"I'm doing well. We are on the campaign trail again today."

"Will it be a crazy day for you?"

"Shouldn't be too bad, we only have two events today. The first is a pancake feed with the Rotary Club in Red Wing. The second is a meeting with some business owners down in Winona."

"Sounds like fun. That reminds me, I still need to take you on the hike up to the top of Barn Bluff in Red Wing. We could get some neat pictures of the Mississippi River up there on a clear day. Also, I've been meaning to go to Winona – there is a company there called Sanborn Canoe Company. They sell artisan axes, and I was hoping to pick one up."

"Count me in for the hike," said Soojin. "I'll keep an eye out for those axes while I'm down here, too. Maybe you can use it on your bachelor trip up to the Boundary Waters with Pete."

"That would be awesome." I had almost forgotten about my upcoming bachelor party. My plan was the opposite of a traditional stag party. Instead of gathering a group of guys and getting a stripper, I had asked my best friend Pete Olson to join me for a fishing trip up in the Boundary Waters Canoe Area. Pete lived close to the BWCA in Ely. We had planned the party around one of his breaks from being deployed overseas as a security contractor with the military.

"What are you up to now?" Soojin asked.

"I'm finally getting out of a traffic jam and trying to make a 9 am meeting for the drug story."

I told Soojin about my conversations with Jesse and Sosa, including the part about being on Smokey's "list."

Soojin drew in her breath. Then she said, "Hun, the way I look at it, you have two choices. You can either lay low and hope the law enforcement agencies are successful in their investigation, or you can double down and help put these thugs behind bars for all of the terrible things they've done to people in this state, including your friend, Ricky."

That was why I loved this woman so much.

"When you put it like that, it's a no brainer. I choose the second option. Plus, with your killer martial arts skills there is nothing I need to worry about, right?"

Soojin laughed. "As long as you are on the campaign trail with me, I can protect you. If you choose to wander afar, I can't be liable for your safety. Especially if you get mixed in with some Republicans along the way."

I chuckled. "Okay, I'll keep you posted on my trip up to Bemidji for the interview, and I'll let you know if anything else comes up. In the meantime, eat some pancakes for me and enjoy your day on the Knutson campaign trail."

"Are you wearing your Knutson 2014 button to work today?"

"I would rather wear a Soojin 2018 one. The first female Governor of Minnesota. And, if you were the Governor, that would make me the ..."

"To quote one of your favorite politicians, Sarah Palin once referred to her husband as Alaska's 'First Dude.' I think that has a good ring to it."

I laughed so hard I nearly missed my turn. "All right, I have to go. I love you, Ms. Governor."

"I love you too, Mr. First Dude."

Chapter 9

Plymouth, MN

I pulled into the parking lot at the Plymouth Drug Addiction Rehabilitation Center at exactly 8:59 am. The campus looked like some kind of merger between a hospital and a high school. It was set on a secluded area surrounded by trees, not far from the appropriately named Medicine Lake. Recovering addicts from throughout the state of Minnesota went there to heal.

I stepped into the reception area, which was immaculate. Beautifully carved stones were embedded into the wall around a cozy fireplace. Comfortable looking couches sat waiting for guests.

The director of the Center greeted me a few minutes later, telling me the group would be ready at 9:30 am. This gave me the chance to take a quick tour of the facility, first. The Center was fully equipped with a dining hall, a patio, meeting rooms, lecture halls, meditation rooms, music and art studios, a gymnasium, bedrooms, and common area lounges, all surrounded by nature. Everything needed was within reach for addicts to recover in their own ways.

At the end of the tour, the director shuttled me into a small group room, where five patients were sitting in a semi-circle facing a single empty chair. The director introduced me as Mr. Cooper Smith, a radio reporter from MPR news. They greeted me warmly, and I thanked them for their time and their courage in sharing their stories with me. The director stepped out, leaving just the six of us.

I gave them some additional background information about myself, and told them how the interview would flow. Once all the administrative details were settled, I placed my voice recorder on a table in the middle of the room. I extended my thumb up to see if everyone was ready. Once all five of their thumbs were up, I hit the record button.

"I'm sitting here today at the Plymouth Drug Addiction Rehabilitation Center with five courageous people. They come from different parts of Minnesota, but they share a common story. This is a story of their addiction to the drug known as heroin. Could everyone please say your first name, age, and where you are from?"

"Aaron, 24, and I'm from Saint Cloud."

"Patrick, 45, from Crookston."

"Elizabeth, 33, and I'm from Eden Prairie."

"Steve, 21, from Moorhead."

"Kelly, 28, and I'm from Rochester."

"Thank you all for agreeing to meet with me today. I know you have all suffered through difficult addictions, and I'd like to ask you a few questions so our listeners can understand the true effects of using heroin."

"First question: how bad is the heroin problem in Minnesota right now?"

"It's crazy." Aaron sat up straighter from his slouched position as he answered. He wore a St. Cloud State University t-shirt and had a tattoo on his inner forearm of the outline of the state of Minnesota.

"It's everywhere," added Elizabeth. She was wearing all black, and had long, black hoop earrings. Although she was thirty-three, she looked like she could have been in her mid-forties.

"You wouldn't believe the people who are using it," said Steve.

"What type of people?" I asked.

"Regular people. The kind you might run into at the grocery store or post office. People from good families," replied Steve.

Steve also wore a university t-shirt, this one for the Dragons football team of Minnesota State University of Moorhead. I wondered if he had been a lineman, given his stout build. He wore a massive sports watch on his left wrist.

"What led you all to heroin? Is there a gateway drug?"

"Prescription pills," said Kelly.

"Which ones?"

"Vicodin for me," Kelly replied, chewing her gum. Her frizzy bleach blonde hair shot out in all directions.

"OxyContin," said Patrick. The others nodded their heads.

Patrick looked like he had just come in from plowing the fields. He wore a John Deere trucker hat and cowboy boots.

"How do you go from prescription pills to heroin?"

"People think prescription pills are harmless, and that they make you feel calm and relaxed," said Elizabeth. "Then, they either become too hard to get, or too expensive. At that point, I switched to dope."

"I started by taking Vicodin every day," said Aaron. He looked down at the tattoo on his arm while he spoke, refusing to make eye contact. "Then, I needed more so I tried taking OxyContin. When that was no longer sustainable, someone offered me heroin. I was reluctant at first, because I am from a good family, and I'm no junkie. But, I couldn't say no. I was already physically addicted to the opium, and I couldn't stand to face the withdrawal."

"One of my friends in high school had serious medical problems," said Steve. "The doctors gave him all sorts of pain medicine. He shared OxyContin with me, and that's how I got hooked." Steve began twisting the watch on his wrist.

"Elizabeth, you said the prescription pills got too expensive, but how much does heroin cost?" I asked.

"As cheap as five dollars a bag," she replied.

"The same price as a pack of Marlboro Reds," said Patrick.

"Heroin is as easy to find as weed. People deal it all across Minnesota in the parking lots of every Walmart and Dairy Queen," said Aaron.

"The best product on the market can go up to twenty dollars for a bag," said Steve.

"What is the best product out there right now?"

"Brown Sugar," replied Steve.

"What makes it the best?"

"People say it's the purest product you can find. It gives you the best high."

"How do you usually consume it?"

"Everyone starts by snorting it," said Aaron. "It's in a powder form, and you snort it like cocaine. After that, most people switch to injecting."

"Why injecting?"

"The rush you get when it hits your veins is euphoric," said Kelly.

"Once you shoot it, there is no going back to sniffing it," said Patrick. He took his trucker hat off and set it on his lap, revealing a pasty white forehead that clashed with his tan cheeks and nose.

"Nothing in the whole world feels as good as injecting heroin, especially the first time," said Aaron.

The group fell silent. Most of them had a faraway look in their eyes, as if they had all gone back to that first big high. I shifted in my chair uncomfortably.

"How much were you doing per day?" I asked, breaking into their reminiscences.

"With the cheaper bags, the five-dollar variety, I could do up to forty bags per day. A 200-a-day habit," said Kelly.

"With the better product, like Brown Sugar, you end up doing around ten hits per day," said Aaron. "At twenty dollars a pop, that is still a 200-a-day habit."

"What did a normal day look like for you when you were using it?"

"My whole day was a quest to find the drug or to find money to buy more of it," said Steve.

"The only thing in life that mattered was the drug," said Patrick.

"What does the high feel like?"

"It's incredible," said Elizabeth. She fiddled with her earrings while she talked. "I can't explain how good it felt."

"Nothing comes close to it. Not prescription drugs, alcohol, or even sex," added Aaron.

"What about the low?"

"Worst feeling in the whole world," said Kelly.

"When I'm low, I just want to die," said Steve.

"There is an unbelievable physical craving," said Patrick. He started tapping the heel of his right cowboy boot on the floor.

"At a certain point, you don't use it to get high – you use it just to function and survive," said Elizabeth.

"I used to fall asleep high, and in the middle of the night when the high would go away, it would wake me up," said Aaron. "I would have to inject again to get back to sleep."

"What about your families and friends? How did your addiction impact your relationship with them?"

"I had to lie to them constantly," said Steve. "I would inject in some random place like a city park in the afternoon. By the time I woke up, it would be dark and I would stumble home to my family."

"Stealing money from my family was the only way I could support my habit," said Elizabeth.

"My six-year-old daughter found my needles and my spoon," said Kelly. She munched harder on her chewing gum. "She showed them to my mother, who tried everything she could think of to get me to stop. She kept telling me I was a terrible influence on my daughter, but I just didn't care. I mean, I loved my daughter, and I obviously still do, but I needed the physical high."

"One of my closest friends overdosed while shooting up with me," said Patrick.

"I talked one of my friends into trying heroin," said Aaron still not looking up. "He ended up sharing a needle with someone who had HIV. Now my friend has AIDs, and it's all my fault."

"Why did you stop?"

"I was arrested," said Aaron.

"To regain custody of my daughter," added Kelly.

"What about the treatment? Why come to this Center here in Plymouth for help?"

"To save my life," said Patrick.

"To reduce my sentence, and possibly avoid jail," said Aaron.

"Was the high worth it?" I asked.

"No," said Patrick. "What is the point of ruining my life over a high you get one day, followed by sickness the next?"

"I never, ever, thought I would be a junkie," said Steve. "It's depressing."

"Will any of you use it again once you are out?"

"I pray every day that I won't go back to that life," said Patrick.

"I can't use it again," said Elizabeth. "If I did, it would kill me."

"What would you tell someone listening who is thinking about trying prescription pills or heroin for the first time?"

"Don't do it!" Kelly yelled as she tightly balled up a handful of her hair.

The room grew absolutely silent. Everyone nodded in agreement, and I could see the pain in their eyes.

Kelly let go of her hair and her arms fell to her lap. "Just don't ever do it," she repeated, softer this time, with tears in her eyes.

Chapter 10

Minneapolis, MN

Jimmy chewed on a toothpick as he drove his Cadillac south down Hennepin Avenue. He crossed Thirty-Sixth Street West and entered the Lakewood Cemetery. The cemetery grounds were open for another thirty-two minutes, and he was instructed to meet Agent Sosa behind the Memorial Chapel in exactly two of those minutes. Things hadn't gone according to his plan recently, and Jimmy knew Sosa would not be happy about it.

Jimmy spotted the large chapel on his left; Sosa said he couldn't miss it with all its red domes. Those red domes were fading to black with the setting sun. Jimmy turned behind the chapel, and sure enough, the same Ford Crown Victoria he was detained in at the Wisconsin Dells was parked right there. Sosa was sitting in the driver's seat by himself. Jimmy pulled up. As instructed, he turned off the vehicle and got into the passenger seat next to Sosa.

"Jimmy, what happened?" asked Sosa as soon as he closed the door. "You said you would give us the whole network on this last shipment. Not only did you fail in that part of the operation, but now at least two kilos of heroin have entered the market, and I have nothing to show for it."

"No, man, you have it wrong." Jimmy took his toothpick out of his mouth. "I never said I would give you the whole network on this last shipment. I said I would try to convince Smokey to send two guys, one to each reservation with a kilo of Brown Sugar. As we discussed in the Dells, I went straight back to Smokey from Wisconsin and told him to send two drivers instead of one for security reasons. He thought about it, but made other plans to send Tank by himself. I wasn't involved, so Smokey never shared the details with me."

"I thought you were his most trusted man. What happened to that?"

"Look, Smokey trusts me completely, but sometimes he just does things without consulting me. What am I supposed to do?"

"You botched this. Things could get a lot worse for you now in the eyes of the federal government," Sosa said.

"Wait a second. There is some good news – two things, in fact. First, Tank was pulled over by a state trooper up on Highway 59 after he was heading north out of Mahnomen. Tank gave the trooper some lip, and his vehicle was searched. Tank said the trooper nearly found the hidden compartment where he was hiding the product. He had his gun ready to waste the guy. Then, Tank saw there was backup coming. When Tank told Smokey about the incident, Smokey called me into his office and told me on the next shipment he would implement the two-man rule. He wants Marcus and I to make the deliveries. That is your chance to do it."

"This is good news," said Sosa, relaxing a bit. "When is the next shipment?"

"Smokey told me the guys in Chicago are running behind on getting the product up from Mexico. Captain told Smokey we won't be able to get the next shipment until the third or fourth week of August, a little over a month from now."

"I want the exact date and location of the deliveries as soon as you find out about them," said Sosa. "Now, what was the second piece of good news?"

Jimmy pulled the recorder out of his pocket and handed it to Sosa.

"I got Smokey on tape talking about his supplier, Captain, in Chicago. He also confirmed his relationship to his two biggest dealers. Their names are Jason Red Eagle on Red Lake, and Jonathan Mason on White Earth. From those two men, the entire Indian nation in northern Minnesota is supplied with Brown Sugar. It's all on the tapes. Smokey even bragged that no police officer could ever touch him now because there is no way anyone would care about the drug problem on those reservations."

"Good job, Jimmy. At least you got the recording part right, that's a step in the right direction. Now that we have this, the primary thing we need you to do is deliver the next shipment with Marcus. We can't wait any longer than next month, nor can we tolerate any additional heroin out on the market."

"Got it, man. Just make sure you come through on your end so I don't end up six feet under in that empty burial plot I passed on the way in."

"Don't worry. As part of the resettlement package, Uncle Sam has thrown in a pre-paid burial plot for you up near your new home in Anchorage, Alaska," Sosa said with a snicker. "It's redeemable at any time, but I personally hope you don't have to use it until you are a prune of an old man. Just make sure that when you do pass away, you go in the summer. The ground is frozen solid up there in the winter, and it would be hard to dig you a proper hole."

"Are we done here?" Jimmy said.

"Sure. We're done. Just come through this time, and I'll see what I can do to get you somewhere warm, like California or Florida. How do those states sound to you?"

"Okay, man, you get me Florida and I'll get you Smokey's whole network. Similar to Alaska, Florida has no state income tax. And, if I'm going to lose my life over your take-down, I'd rather go down dreaming of beautiful women in bikinis on a tax-free Miami beach instead of Eskimos in parkas up in Alaska."

"I'll make some calls and see what I can do on Florida for you. Just get me Smokey and his network."

"I will," said Jimmy, getting out of the car.

He started to head toward his Cadillac when he heard Sosa roll down his window and call for him.

"Hey, Jimmy. I got something for you," said Sosa.

When Jimmy turned back to the car, Sosa handed him a small piece of tan leather.

"What's this?"

"It's a classy toothpick holder, made by Leather Works in Saint Paul. I thought you should start carrying your toothpicks around in style."

Jimmy put it in his pocket, shaking his head as he turned away from Sosa. That was all the fun he could take for one night.

He watched Agent Sosa drive his vehicle away. The cemetery was about to close in a few minutes, and it was getting dark and a bit unsettling to be among the dead at night. Once Sosa was out of sight, Jimmy jumped into his Cadillac and turned on the interior lights. He grabbed the toothpick holder out of one pocket and fished some toothpicks out of his other one. He put a new toothpick in his mouth and placed a few others in his new holder. He held the new toothpick holder under the light. *Not bad, actually. I can work with this.*

Except, that toothpick holder would be a constant reminder that he would soon have to help take down Smokey and the whole crew. Was he conflicted? Maybe he had been before now – but staying out of prison and getting a new life in Florida? Well, Jimmy could get used to that.

Sorry, Smokey. You're going down.

Chapter 11

Saint Paul, MN

A few weeks had passed since Jesse said he would try to get Roy Cloud for an interview, but he had yet to deliver. It was early August already, and although I had a decent overview of Smokey and his network, I still needed a well-placed source to make the story complete. Roy Cloud was the man who could map out the flow of the drugs from Jason Red Eagle on down throughout the entire reservation. *Where is Roy Cloud? Is he on the run? Is he dead in a ditch somewhere?*

I was pondering these questions while enjoying a warm caramel roll and a black cup of coffee at Keys Café on Roberts Street, a few blocks away from MPR headquarters. I was scheduled to meet with Bill in his office later today to talk about the story, but I knew I needed more for him. I couldn't stomach another Wild Bill blow-up today.

My mind had now shifted from Roy Cloud to Agent Sosa, who I hoped would be more willing to share details with me about the case. I had not talked to him since he told me I was on Smokey's list. I knew he wasn't excited about my involvement, but I wanted to show him I could be a force multiplier for his investigation.

I fished my iPhone out of my pocket and scrolled through my contacts down to Sosa. Before I could push the call button, my screen lit up with an incoming call – from none other than Jesse himself.

"This must be my lucky day," I said answering on the first ring.

"Why, yes, Coop. As a matter of fact, you are in luck," said Jesse. "I finally got in touch with Cloud, and he agreed to meet with you. I told him if he cooperated with you, I would see what I could do about easing up on him for a while."

"Jesse, that's such good news. Thank you."

"Before we go any further, you must understand that Cloud demanded absolutely no police involvement with the interview. He said if he even sees one cop on patrol in the same town you meet in he will leave immediately. That means this all has to happen under the radar. It also means I won't be involved in the actual meeting. It'll just be you and Cloud and whoever else he decides to bring."

"Are you saying I'll be in danger?"

"Cloud will likely come by himself, because there is no point in him highlighting his relationship with you to anyone else in his tribe. However, Red Eagle and Smokey have guys everywhere, and I mean everywhere. You have to be very careful about where and when you meet."

"What do you suggest?"

"Well, it will be suspicious if Cloud travels too far from the reservation, so preferably you would meet someplace close to, but not in, Bemidji. There are too many police officers roaming around Bemidji. Some of the small towns nearby would be much better for a meeting."

"You know the area way better than I do. What do you recommend?"

"I thought you would say that, so I did some brainstorming. There is a small town just west of Bemidji called Bagley. It's located right on Highway 2. It's roughly forty-five minutes away from the reservation. There is a place you can rent out called The Farm by the Lake. It's a secluded farmhouse on Lake Lomond. You could go there, rent the place out, and have him show up after dark. You do the interview, and he leaves. You stay overnight and take off the next morning."

"Sounds perfect, thanks. How do I arrange this, logistically?"

"I have Cloud's email. I'll send it to you after this call. You send Cloud an email that says you're 'a friend of Jesse,' and he'll respond. Send him the date, time, and location. Let me know the exact details, and I can be just down the road on Lake Lomond Drive with my off-duty vehicle, in case there is trouble."

"That all sounds good, Jesse, except the part about you being there. If this goes south, I don't want you to get caught up in it."

"It's too dangerous for you to do alone."

"Don't worry, I have someone else I can ask for backup."

"Who?"

"None other than Pete Olson," I said with a grin.

"Pete Olson! Like, Navy SEAL Pete Olson?" Jesse yelled.

I imagined Jesse's eyes wide with surprise. "Ex-Navy SEAL Pete Olson now," I said. "He left the Navy last year and now he is contracting for Uncle Sam, making ten times his former military salary on three-month trips to the warzones in the Middle East."

"No kidding. So where is he living now?

"He is living up in Ely."

"All right, I feel comfortable if he has your back. I will plan to stay away during the meeting. Let me know if you need anything else."

"Thanks, I owe you big time."

"That's right, you do. I want you to come wash and wax my fishing boat and patrol car on your way back from the meeting. No spots on there – that wax finish better shine."

"Real funny, Jesse. Just send me Cloud's email."

***

I quickly finished off my coffee and took off on foot for work. I was jazzed, both with the news and with the caffeine running through my body. The timing was perfect, too, as I had already lined up my bachelor party with Pete the following weekend. If Cloud was available, I could just change our trip location from Ely to Bagley and everything would fall into place – as long as Pete was okay with it.

I could have taken the back entrance to MPR on Ninth Street, but I needed to keep up my daily news ticker ritual at the main entrance. Even when it was thirty below zero in January I would stop and read the first headline. I rounded the corner onto Cedar Street and stopped to read today's.

> *Friday, August 8, 2014 –*
> *Obama Authorizes Airstrikes*
> *Against ISIS Insurgents in*
> *Northern Iraq...*

Great, back in Iraq. It seemed like my whole life I had been watching events unfold in Iraq. I was fourteen months old when Operation Desert Storm kicked off in January of 1991. I don't remember specific highlights from the Gulf War, but my father still joked about how glued I was to the television during the nightly news updates from the front lines. Then there was the "Shock and Awe" bombing campaign of Baghdad during Operation Iraqi Freedom in 2003, followed by the hanging of Saddam Hussein in December 2006, and the eventual U.S. military withdrawal in 2011. *Iraq, give us all a break already.*

I made it up to the third floor and found my desk in the cubicle farm. Lisa had her back to me, typing away on her computer. I threw my bag down loud enough to get

Lisa's attention. Her body didn't move but her head cocked to the side. She stared at me with a look that screamed, *I am annoyed at you for breathing my same air, Cooper Smith.*

"Happy Friday, Lisa."

"Don't even start with me," she said, looking back at her screen.

"You sure are chipper today. Did you just find out you were from Wisconsin or what?"

"Good one, ginger."

Lisa never hesitated to make fun of my red-tinted hair and beard. I decided to ignore her; she had no clue about my upcoming interview with Cloud.

"Hey, Bill's been over twice already looking for you," she said. "You better get in his office soon."

"Thanks for the heads up."

I looked over and saw Bill motioning me to his office with his index finger like a father does to a disobedient child right before he reprimands him. I walked straight into his office.

"Close the door and sit down, Cooper," said Bill matter-of-factly.

"Sure thing. You wanted to see me?"

"We need to talk about the Brown Sugar story. We need to either push ahead with it, or nix it and move on. I have money allocated for it, but the sharks are circling."

"I just made a big break in the story. My connection in Bemidji secured a meeting for me with a source inside the Red Lake reservation drug network. The source has agreed to give me a tell-all exclusive interview next weekend."

"That's what I wanted to hear. If it's a good interview, you should be able to piece that together with what you already have and we can go live with it."

"What about the DEA's demand for us to wait?"

"We've waited long enough."

"I know, but remember they caught me with that Brown Sugar packet. I don't want to go to jail."

Bill started laughing, and soon his whole body shook. I had never actually seen him laugh, and I had a feeling he only did so when it was cynical in nature.

"What's so funny?"

"I'm picturing you in an orange jump suit in the prison cafeteria waiting for the cook to slop down your liquid mash potatoes as you stand in line next to Smokey."

"Come on, this is serious," I said. "Can we wait for the DEA to take Smokey's crew down first before running the story?"

"Do you think I care about the DEA and their schedule? Have they even given you any concrete details about the investigation?" Bill paused to let his rhetorical question hang in the air. "No, of course not. I know you had that terrible slip of the hand, but it's time for you to finish this story. There are plenty of ambitious reporters out there on the streets collecting food stamps who would love to be in your shoes. Do you want to join them?"

"No, of course not."

"I'm starting to think this story isn't worth my time anymore. Maybe we should just cut it right here, right now."

"Bill, I understand the DEA has taken its time – but this story could be worthy of a Peabody. Think about it. We will be exposing a major drug ring in Minnesota, highlighting the effects of heroin on people from all across our great state, and taking down a big-time supplier of the product. This is big league material, and, of course, as my managing editor, you'll be recognized too when we win the Peabody."

I had purposely never used the P word with Bill. I knew how badly he wanted another one. MPR had won several Peabody Awards over the years, but they were tough as hell to get.

"We have the series about the Catholic Church we ran last month," countered Bill. "If anything, that will win the Peabody."

"Yes, but you didn't play a key role in that one, and your name won't be listed," I countered. "Why not double down our chances with this story? If we run it at the end of this month, we can have a second solid entry for the 2014 Peabodies."

"Cooper, don't you dare push my buttons," Bill said, wagging a finger at me. "I admit, you have a good story, but I'm not in the business of waiting around. Especially for the federal government. Get a solid interview and share the highlights with the DEA. Use that as leverage to get the DEA to move faster on their investigation."

"I'll make it happen."

"Good, now get out of my sight before I put Lisa on this story once and for all."

I was out of his office faster than a deep fried cheese curd goes down a throat at the Minnesota State Fair.

***

I was smiling ear-to-ear as I walked out of MPR headquarters that evening. I sent Cloud an email that afternoon, and received a quick email confirmation from him agreeing to meet for the interview, just as Jesse had promised he would. I made my reservations at the Farm by the Lake, and I was ready to interview Cloud next weekend.

I decided to celebrate so I called Soojin to surprise her with dinner reservations at the historic Saint Paul Hotel, a landmark in the city since 1910. The hotel was home to Soojin's favorite restaurant, the Saint Paul Grill.

We sat in our usual table. I ordered the filet mignon, and she ordered the salmon. We shared a bottle of Malbec wine from Argentina as we waited for our food.

"How's the campaign going? I saw you are still up ten points in the polls." I cut into my filet. It was cooked perfectly.

"It's chaotic, like usual. Today, at a campaign event in Shakopee, the Governor literally kissed thirty babies. I counted." Soojin finished off her glass of wine.

"That sounds like a pretty easy job. Kissing babies' heads all day. Does it make you want to have kids?"

"Maybe we could just adopt a child who is already past the baby and toddler stages. I'm thinking between the age of three and four. They would have to come potty-trained, though." Soojin winked.

I laughed. "Sounds like a good idea to me." I set down my fork. "You know, I'm a little nervous about my upcoming trip."

"Your bachelor party with Pete? Are you afraid the fish won't bite?"

I filled her in on the change of plans, including the details about the interview with Cloud. When I finished, Soojin pulled out her iPhone and showed me a picture of an axe with a big red ribbon on it. My bunched up shoulders fell, and I relaxed for the first time that day.

"It's for you. I picked it up when I was down in Winona and wanted to give it to you for your upcoming trip. Maybe the axe can help you feel safer. Or, at the very least, I'm sure you could find some firewood to chop while you are waiting for your interview to start."

"Thanks! I feel safer already. Where is the axe?"

"It's at my apartment; you can pick it up on the way home."

"Probably best that you didn't bring it to dinner; I wouldn't want people to think I was an axe murderer or something." I stuck my tongue out at her. "Hey, have you decided what you are going to do for your bachelorette party?"

"I talked to Jill today, and the over-achieving maid of honor said we are definitely going to order some male strippers."

I set down my glass of wine. "Really?"

"I'm just messing with you. Actually, she did confirm she is taking me to Hastings for the day."

"Real funny joke!" I took a big swig of wine. "You know; I'd be okay with the strippers if that is what she had planned."

"Sure you would…" Soojin rolled her eyes.

"What's in Hastings?" I asked.

"There's this place that lets you take construction equipment like bulldozers and excavators out to a giant sandbox to play in. Apparently, there is a fire truck involved, too."

"That sounds pretty epic. Do you think the fire truck comes with male strippers dressed like firefighters?"

Soojin laughed. "I guess I'll find out soon enough – it's next weekend."

I sighed. "Well, at least one of us will have an exciting last hurrah."

Chapter 12

Ely, MN

The outdoorsy town of Ely was known for being the launch-off point for excursions into the Boundary Waters Canoe Area within the Superior National Forest in northeast Minnesota. The BWCA covered well over a million acres of some of the most scenic waterways and wildlife in America. No power motorboats were allowed in the area, making for a serene experience that was near therapeutic for some.

Pete and I had originally planned to spend three days up in the BWCA, but my upcoming meeting with Roy Cloud changed our plans. I rolled into town on a Friday afternoon after a four-hour drive up from Saint Paul, and I was looking forward to a peaceful night at Pete's cabin before heading out to Bagley the next day.

I called Pete when I was close, and he told me to meet him downtown at the Boathouse Brewpub on Highway 169 and First Avenue. I scored a nearby parking spot on the street and entered the pub. It had wood-finished walls and smelled of grease and beer. *Exactly what I wanted.* I had arrived between the lunch and dinner crowd, and the place was nearly empty.

As Pete stood up from a table to greet me, I stared for a moment. I had kept in close email and phone contact with Pete over the years, but he didn't post images of himself online. He was away on work so much it had been almost a year since our last get-together. I noticed he had continued to pack on the muscle. When Pete went into the Navy out of high school, he was a tall, wiry kid, with an awkward disposition and little-to-no muscle. After six years with the Navy SEALs, he was now a jacked warrior. Standing well over six feet tall, he looked like Captain America. His neck and shoulders were bulging out of his t-shirt, and his legs filled out his blue jeans. He wore a Carhartt baseball cap over short brown hair. He had bright blue eyes, which had won over all the ladies back in school. His beard looked about a week old, and he had a smashed-in nose – the kind of nose one gets from being a knuckle-dragger in one crappy warzone after the next with the SEALs.

"Pete, you're like the incredible hulk! You're making me feel small," I said, giving him a "bro-hug" consisting of a hand clasp, followed by a torso lean toward each other, and a final, sturdy pat on the back.

"Coop, you son of a gun," said Pete. "It's great to see you. How long has it been? A full year now?"

"Too long my friend. It's great to see you, too. Let's order some food and drinks –we have a lot to catch up on."

"Sounds good, my man."

We ordered the pub's signature beer-battered walleye and two blueberry blonde ales. We sat back and smiled.

"So, tell me, Pete. How much can you bench press now at the gym?"

"That's easy. Just count however much you can do, and double it. Same goes for the squat lift."

"How do you like being out of the Navy?"

"It's great. I'm making big bucks now working only six months out of the year. The rest of the time I get to hang out in my sweet cabin with my family. The days are filled with fishing and hunting. Best of all, I'm away from the crowds. How about you?"

"That sounds pretty amazing," I said. "Things are well. Soojin and I are ready to get married and start our lives together in Saint Paul."

"Congrats. I'm happy for you."

"Thanks. How are Brittany and Jack doing?"

"They are both doing well. Brittany is loving being a mother, and she is great at it. She is also busy gearing up for the next basketball season. Jack is finally sleeping through the night, so we are happy campers."

"That's awesome."

"How is work going for you?" Pete asked.

"Work has been challenging. I hope this interview in Bagley helps raise my stock at MPR a bit. This is the one I told you about the other day on the phone."

"I bet if you do well, they will offer you Garrison Keillor's show when he retires. Do you ever talk to him?"

I'd already received dozens of questions about this in the past year. Garrison Keillor was a Minnesota legend whose story-telling was world famous. His show was broadcast across America to nearly every public radio station via *NPR*.

"I've met him a few times. He is actually a down-to-earth guy, and you can't beat the *Prairie Home Companion* show."

"I feel like I'm living in Lake Wobegon every day of my life," Pete said with a satisfied sigh.

"Sometimes I envy people like you for that," I said. "But I enjoy living in the Twin Cities and being part of the hustle and bustle."

"Amen, for people like you, but that's definitely not for me. So, what's the new plan for this weekend? I was really looking forward to going up to the BWCA to catch some fish."

"Yeah, sorry for the last minute change of plans. As I mentioned last week on the phone, I'm working a huge story about this big heroin ring in Minnesota and I now have a source inside the network willing to meet me tomorrow night in Bagley. I wanted to ask you a huge favor."

"Let me guess, you are in need of a little steel?" Pete flexed his biceps.

"Yes, but I feel terrible even asking. I know you have responsibilities here with your family and I don't want to pull you away from them. Especially to work."

"No worries, my man. I have to keep my skills sharp in between contract jobs out in my favorite Middle Eastern playgrounds. I just want to know who we are dealing with so I can bring the right equipment."

"I can pay you for your time. Maybe not what you bill Uncle Sam, but quote me a price and I'll see what I can do to get you the money."

Pete waved a hand dismissively. "Nonsense. I still owe you for lining up my first date with Brittany. She is the best thing to happen to me, and she gave me a strong and healthy baby boy. Besides, it will probably be pretty low key in Bagley, right?"

I proceeded to fill Pete in on everything I knew about Smokey and his network. We ate delicious Boathouse food and gulped down even better beer as we talked through the specifics of the interview and location. As we talked, I was still amazed at his physique, and some small part of me wished I had signed up years ago with the Navy, too. Especially right now.

**

After dinner, I got back into Wellstone and followed Pete out to his cabin. There was still plenty of sunlight left in the day, and Pete promised me some fishing before the sun dropped beyond the western horizon. He had a cozy log cabin on three acres nestled up to Shagawa Lake, directly across from the Grand Lodge, a resort on the edge of Ely.

I parked Wellstone, and Brittany walked up to us with little Jack in her arms. She still looked like the stellar athlete I'd always known her to be. She grew up just down the street from me, and we shot hoops together as kids. She was the only black girl in our high school, which couldn't have been easy for her. She threw herself into basketball her freshmen year, and she never looked back. By the end of our senior year, she had led the Duluth East Greyhounds basketball team to a state title.

She went on to play for the UMD Bulldogs on a full ride. It gave me four more years to cheer for her as she dominated the hardwood. After college, she moved up to Ely to coach the women's basketball team at Vermillion Community College. When Pete told me he wanted to move to Ely after the Navy, I made sure to connect them. That high school reunion had quickly turned into marriage and a family. I couldn't be happier for them.

"Coach Olson! It's great to see you again. Jack is a handsome little devil."

"Thanks, Coop." Brittany handed Jack to me. "When are you and Soojin going to make one of these?"

He was heavier than I expected. "One step at a time. First comes the marriage, then the honeymoon, then we will talk about kids. How is your team looking for the upcoming season?"

"We have three returning starters who are all excellent players. We hope to do well this year, and build off of last year's successful season."

"That's great. Do you ever miss playing?"

"Sure, everyone does. I still am young enough to run around with these women. But, my passion is coaching. And, now I have other priorities." Brittany took Jack back from me when he started to fuss. "I can't blow out a knee and expect to carry this guy around."

"Tell me about it, he's heavy."

"Come on," said Pete. "Let's try to catch some fish before the sun sets on us."

We headed straight out to Pete's dock with a couple of fishing poles. We planned to take the boat out but decided we would cast off the dock instead. I hadn't fished in a while, so it took me a few casts to get my rhythm back.

"Coop," Pete said as he sent his line sailing out to the water, "did you bring any weapons with you for the trip?"

I paused and laughed a bit before saying, "You'll make fun of me."

"What, did you bring a pocket knife or a paintball gun or something?"

"I know you're a Republican, and I also know you are a well-trained killing machine. You are an expert marksman and I have no problem with you owning any type of firearm or weapon out on the market. I, on the other hand, am a card-carrying Democrat for the MN-DFL. I don't own a single firearm. Plus, I just don't see the point in having one down in the Twin Cities."

Pete shook his head. "You're crazy. If I lived down there I would have way more fire-power than what I have out here in the sticks. But I get it, gun control and all that for you card-carrying hippie."

We both laughed.

"Seriously, though, what equipment did you bring?"

"Well, I really only have my axe; it's like a tomahawk-type thing," I said.

Pete busted out in laughter that echoed across the lake. "Where did you ever buy a tomahawk from?"

"Soojin picked it up for me from the Sanborn Canoe Company down in Winona. It's called the Hudson Bay Camp Axe, and it's got a sweet Indian feather design on it," I said, chuckling.

"Coop, have you stopped to think about this for a second? You are meeting with an Indian drug dealer, close to two reservations, and you are bringing a tomahawk for protection. The very weapon the Chippewa tribe mastered centuries before you were born…"

"Okay, I get your point, but it's all I have. It's not like I was planning on using it." My line jerked. "Got one. Looks like a nice little walleye."

"Saved by the fish, let me get the net." Pete leaned over to get a better look at my catch. "Looks like it's just a little guy like you." Pete laughed. "Toss it back."

After I got the hook out, I tossed the fish back in the water and looked over at Pete.

"What about you? What kind of weapons do you plan to bring?"

"I want to be ready for anything, but I think my hunting rifle and sidearm should do the trick – with a ton of ammo on hand, of course. I'll also have some other tactical gear on standby."

"Great, thanks for having my back on this. I don't expect anything to happen, but I'm glad you'll be around."

Pete started to chuckle again.

"What's so funny?" I asked.

His laughter grew louder.

"Come on, Pete, what's so funny?"

"This is supposed to be your bachelor party, right? I'm just picturing you pulling your little tomahawk out of your bag and swinging it away at some Indian like you know how to use it!" Pete made a mock swinging motion with his fishing rod.

"All right, all right, laugh it up. Any man can kill with a gun, but a real man kills with an axe," I said, smiling.

"Okay, Crazy Horse, you get that tomahawk blade nice and sharp as a last-resort weapon. But, let's hope no one gets killed so you can get your interview and become the next Garrison Keillor!"

It was my turn to swing my fishing rod like a battle-axe, and we both laughed long and loud all the way into the night. I fell into a deep sleep the moment my head hit the pillow. Little did I know it would be my last good night's rest for quite some time.

Chapter 13

Bagley, MN

It was my second four-hour car ride of the weekend. We drove from Pete's house in Ely to the Farm by the Lake in Bagley. This time I left Wellstone in Ely and rode along with Pete in his blue Chevy pickup truck. We stopped once in Bemidji at the Paul Bunyan and Babe the Blue Ox statue, partly to stretch our legs, but mainly to rub Bunyan's big black boots for good luck.

We rolled into Bagley in the afternoon. The green population sign read 1,392. The meeting with Roy Cloud was scheduled for 9 pm that night, so we had a few hours to kill.

The Farm by the Lake was a non-profit retreat on Lake Lomond. A Bagley native who wanted to provide a space to help people get away from the daily grind gifted it to the community in 1983. The farm was set on a large plot of land, mostly wooded, with a few well-mowed areas to play sports and lawn games.

As we drove down the Farm's gravel driveway, Pete started nodding his head and saying things like, "Good terrain," "great cover," and "nice choke point." His military training was clearly kicking in, and I was glad he could see all the angles, because I certainly could not.

We pulled up to an old bunkhouse. This was where we would be staying and conducting the interview. The caretakers were gone for the weekend, but they had left the key on a hook with a welcome note on the front door.

The bunkhouse had a warm feel to it. It had an open area living room with two lofts overhead. There were a couple of bedrooms off to the left side. In the middle was a fireplace next to a stand-up piano, with old furniture spaced out awkwardly in the room. Above the piano was a photo of an outdoorsy man in a tan hat and bright red shirt and coat, a kind smile on his face. He stood in front of a lake with two geese swimming behind him. *A peaceful picture from a different time.* A metal ladder led up to the loft on the left, whereas the loft on the right had regular stairs situated next to a small kitchen and dining table. It was perfect for an interview.

Pete told me he was going to go *secure the perimeter*, whatever that entailed. I decided to walk down to the lake. The Farm had an old wooden dock that stretched from a patch of grass to Lake Lomond. I watched the waves roll in as the wind whipped against my face. I could see a few people out fishing, and one boat pulling inner tubes with screaming kids in them. They had no clue that my guest at the Farm would be a drug dealer, and I wanted to keep it that way.

After a few minutes, Pete called out to me. He needed help setting up some traps as a safety measure. We tied a rope to a large, fallen tree and propped it up against a huge branch next to the driveway. With one pull, the tree could cover the road and impede a vehicle's progress.

Pete found a couple of portable five-gallon tanks full of gasoline in the shed. I started to keep track in my notebook of all the extra expenses we would have to pay the caretakers for. He made several improvised Molotov cocktails with empty beer glass bottles and old rags. He positioned them around the yard and woods in what I could only assume were strategic locations. I was amazed as I watched Pete think and work. He was a machine. I would hate to be on the receiving end of an operation conducted by the Navy SEALs.

After a long afternoon of work, I watched the sun sinking toward the horizon. Cloud was expected to arrive at any moment. Pete checked his rifle and handgun one more time and told me to keep the tomahawk by the rear door, just in case. He also told me not to be a hero. *Don't worry about that, Pete, **you're** the hero,* I thought. He set out for the woods, and I waited in the bunkhouse with the voice recorder ready.

***

Cloud showed up right on time, driving what looked like an orange El Camino. He parked next to Pete's truck and came up to the bunkhouse. He was alone and didn't appear to be armed. I opened the door.

"Hello, Mr. Cloud, thanks for coming."

"Hey, man, are you the reporter?"

"Yes, my name is Cooper Smith, and I'm with Minnesota Public Radio."

"Okay, whatever." He waved a hand dismissively. "Let's get this over with."

"Why don't you come over here and sit down? This should only take an hour or so if you answer all of my questions openly."

"No one is going to find out it was me, right? You're going to do the sound masking thing they do on *60 Minutes* with the weird distorted voice?"

"Yes, I'll record it normally here, and our audio engineers will mask your voice so it's completely unrecognizable. We won't even ask for your name."

"Let's start already."

Roy Cloud was scrappy-looking, and I guessed him to be about thirty. He had long black hair and wore a UFC fighter's shirt. I studied one of the many tattoos on his skin – this one a bird on his neck – wondering whether it was a hawk or an eagle. *Don't stare, Coop,* I told myself.

"Please begin by telling me about Brown Sugar."

"It really caught our tribe off guard. Until Brown Sugar came along, we had a long-established drug trade that was passed down to each new generation. We would buy the heroin from a distributor out east, dilute the product down, and sell it to our addicts. There was a clear pecking order. William Kingbird ran the show, and his son was next in line to the throne. The rest of us fell into place, and we all had our roles. Jason Red Eagle was Kingbird's right-hand man, Matthew Red Bear was in charge of security, and I was one of the dealers. Once Brown Sugar hit the market, everyone wanted the product. We were forced to connect with Smokey. It was the biggest mistake we ever made."

"How so?"

"Can I smoke?"

"Sure, go ahead. Let me get you an ashtray."

Roy pulled out a pack of Winston cigarettes and a lighter. He lit one up and took a long pull. Then he set the cigarette on the corner of the ashtray and leaned back in his chair.

"When the day came for us to buy Brown Sugar, Smokey murdered Kingbird, his son, and Matthew."

"When did that happen?"

"Back in April. Smokey brought his guys up and shot our guys in cold blood. Only Jason got away. He said he was almost shot and narrowly escaped with his life. After that, we were all pretty shook up."

"So, who took over after Kingbird?"

"Jason. He was the next best person for the job."

"How was he able to buy Brown Sugar?"

"Jason knew we would all be in trouble if he didn't sell the product, because it was the best on the market. He told me he personally contacted Smokey a few weeks after the murders, and they cut a deal. Smokey would leave Jason alone to deal on Red Lake, as long as he exclusively sold Brown Sugar. He agreed."

"Do you think it was smart for Jason to cut a deal with the people who killed his former boss?"

Roy took another pull from his burning cigarette. "They also killed Jason's cousin, Matthew. What could he do, though? It was either sell the Brown Sugar product, or get forced out. In Jason's case, he probably would have been killed by Smokey if he didn't go along with it. I don't blame him for making the deal."

"Can you tell me a little bit about your network? Walk me through the whole process, from the beginning, where the product is grown, all the way to your end user."

"I can only tell you a little bit about the front-end side of the business; I mainly deal with the addicts."

"All right."

"Jason told me the product is grown in Mexico by a cartel. It is shipped up to a distribution center in Chicago. From there, it is sold to regional dealers. Smokey is Minnesota's dealer, so he buys the product and sells it to the reservations. Once we get the product, it is given out to us street-level dealers. I am one of five dealers for Red Lake. I had an established network of addicts before Brown Sugar, but since we have been selling it, new customers have been coming to me. Kids as young as fifteen are getting addicted to opium from prescription drugs like OxyContin. It's an easy transition to go up to heroin. With Brown Sugar being so pure, the high is like nothing these kids have ever experienced before. It keeps them coming back for more."

"How many customers do you have?"

Roy closed one eye and looked up toward the ceiling with his other as he counted in his head. "Around sixty, give-or-take."

"How much product do they buy?"

"Most buy five to ten bags per day. At twenty dollars a pop, it's between one to two hundred dollars per customer each day."

I quickly scribbled the math out for 60 x $150 on my notebook. "That's around $9,000 per day?"

"Yeah, on a good day I'll do up to $10,000."

"How can they afford to buy so much?"

Roy crossed his arms and sat back in his chair. "It depends. Some use casino money, but most of the population is poor. They scrape by and sacrifice other parts of their lives so they can do the drug. I give them the product, they give me the cash, and we go our separate ways until I see them again the next day. I don't ask too many questions."

That will make a good sound bite, I thought.

"When do you expect to receive the next shipment from Smokey, and how much will you get?"

"It is supposed to happen real soon, and it will likely be our biggest one yet. At least two, if not three kilos of product."

"Who receives the product from Smokey?"

"Well, Smokey won't bring it up himself. It will probably be one of his guys."

I looked back at my notes. "Earlier in our conversation, you said, 'Smokey is Minnesota's dealer, and he sells the product to the reservations.' What other reservations does he sell to?"

"The only one I know of is White Earth. We have a long history of clashes with them. Jason was mad when he found out Smokey was selling to them too."

"Who runs their operation?"

"Jonathan Mason. He is–"

I heard what sounded like several vehicles rushing down the driveway outside.

"What the hell is that?" Roy asked, shoving his chair back. He pulled a handgun out from behind his back, and sprinted for the door. A few seconds later, I heard the crunch of a vehicle colliding with something, followed by the deafening roar of a high-powered rifle.

I followed Roy out of the bunkhouse. He rushed for his El Camino. I turned left and headed toward the log cabin house. I would have a clear path to look down the driveway, and a supply of at least two Molotov cocktails. As I sprinted toward the corner of the cabin, I heard a loud succession of gunfire. I didn't have the ear to pick up how many there were.

When I safely made the edge of the cabin, I peered around the corner and looked down the driveway. Floodlights had turned on at various points in the driveway, as well as around each of the buildings. By their light, I could see one pickup truck smashed against the fallen tree in the driveway that we had set earlier. The pickup was on fire, and I thought I could make out two bodies burning on the hood of the vehicle. On either side of the driveway were two sedans with people piling out of them. I counted six men.

A moment later, the El Camino came into view. Roy rounded the corner of the driveway by the bunkhouse and accelerated toward the chaos. When he realized the driveway was blocked, he turned right into an open field. He was met with a volley of gunfire from the men who had just arrived and were approaching him. The El Camino stalled. Roy got out and fired his pistol blindly toward the attackers, ducking behind his vehicle for safety.

One of the attackers started dashing toward Roy just as a flash of light came from the woods to the northwest. A loud crack spilt the air as the man was knocked sideways, like he was doing a cartwheel. The remaining five men scampered back around their vehicles to the nearby trees for cover and started shooting northwest into the woods.

I pulled my lighter out of my pocket and fumbled it as I tried lighting one of the Molotov cocktails. *Light, you stupid thing, light.* I jogged northeast of the log cabin toward the community picnic building. I finally lit my cocktail and chucked it as hard and far as I could. It landed behind the woods where the attackers were positioned. The men turned to look in my direction – then opened fire. I ducked behind the picnic building for cover as bullets whizzed by. *So, this was what war was like.*

I caught a quick glimpse of Pete. The diversion had allowed him to get down to the bunkhouse from the woods. I saw his muzzle flash and heard another man go down. The other four were running away. I had my second and last cocktail in my hand. I lit it as I snuck to the far corner of the picnic building. I chucked the cocktail, and it exploded near the men in the woods. I dipped back around for safety.

From my angle, I could see Roy ducked down behind his vehicle. He made it far enough to the edge of his front bumper so that he could shoot toward the attackers. Just beyond Roy was Pete, who was now set up by the log cabin and had a clear line of sight on the assailants. He fired two well-placed rounds back-to-back, and two more of the men collapsed. The remaining two men panicked and split up; one bolted southeast straight toward Roy, and the other headed west into the woods.

Pete disappeared back around the bunkhouse to catch up with the man in the woods, and I came around the other side of the picnic building, ready to dash for safety. *Roy, you better move. Roy, he's coming for you.* The man was sprinting directly for Roy, but there was no way Roy would be able to see him in time from his position. "Look behind you!" I screamed. Roy turned around just in time to shoot the attacker. He went down.

I ran over to Roy. The other man was facedown and not moving.

"Are you okay?" I asked.

Roy stood up and looked out over his car toward the woods. "Yes, thanks for the heads up. Are there any more?"

I looked up to see if I could spot Pete or the last man who had come with the assailants. "I think there is one more."

"Who is killing all these people?"

Before I could respond we both turned our heads slightly, focusing on a specific point in the woods where we heard a loud thud, followed by the sound of a man gasping for air. We then heard a crack, followed by silence.

"I'm getting out of here," said Roy. He jumped in his car and took off down the ditch.

Relief flooded me as Pete walked out of the woods under a floodlight. He was smiling, his demeanor calm, as if he hadn't just killed several men. In his hand was my axe, and it was dripping with blood.

"You have got to be kidding me," I said. "You killed that last dude with my axe?"

"Well, you weren't using it were you?"

"Are you serious? Did you, like, throw it at him, or what?"

"Yeah, just like in the movies. Then I ran up and broke his neck."

A shiver went down my spine because I knew he was dead serious. "Did you learn how to do that back with the SEALs?"

"SEALs possess many skills, one of which is that we can kill a man with just about anything, including your chic tomahawk."

"It's good to have you on Team America, Pete. And, it's good to have you on my team tonight," I said, saluting him. "I wonder who they were…"

Pete saluted me back and walked over to the body next to me. "Who killed this one?"

"Roy Cloud did, just before he bolted."

Pete searched the dead man and found his wallet. He tossed it to me.

I looked inside and found an ID. "White Earth Indian Reservation," I said. "What were these guys doing here?"

"I don't know, but we may want to get out of here before anyone else shows up. You might also want to leave a blank check to pay the caretakers for all of this mess."

"Good idea, let's go."

"Hey, Coop," said Pete as we headed toward his pickup. "Were you able to get your interview?"

I patted my pocket; amazingly, my voice recorder was still there. "Yes," I said. "And with this tape, Smokey's whole network is about to collapse."

"Maybe, but until it does, Smokey is going to send all available resources to take you out once he hears about tonight. You need to find a safe house, and mine won't cut it. You better call that DEA guy right away."

"Okay," I said, as the extent of what had just happened sank in. "I'll give him a call, after I call Jesse and Soojin. What's your plan?"

"Well, as much as I would love to walk away from this, we better tell all of your law enforcement friends what happened. Back to Bemidji?"

I sighed. "Yes. Back to Bemidji."

Pete smiled. "Was this a memorable bachelor party or what?"

"You can bet I'll never forget it. Thanks, Pete."

Chapter 14

Minneapolis, MN

Smokey chucked his phone against the wall of his home office after his call with Jonathan Mason from White Earth. Jimmy, Tank, and Marcus knew something terrible had happened. They nervously waited to hear what the boss had to say.

"Eight of Mason's guys were killed last night in Bagley while trying to take out Roy Cloud and that reporter from MPR," said Smokey, clenching his teeth.

"How is that even possible?" asked Jimmy.

"Apparently, the reporter brought some special forces military guy with him. The trained killer wiped them all out. Eight dead Indians." Smokey shook his head in disbelief.

"So, Cloud and Smith got away?" asked Marcus.

"Yes, and the reporter's military friend, too."

"What are you going to do now, boss?" asked Tank.

"Toss me my phone," said Smokey, holding out his hand toward Marcus. "I'm going to call Jason Red Eagle and ask for updates."

Marcus picked up the phone and was surprised to see it was still intact after hitting the wall. He threw it to Smokey, who dialed Jason, putting the call on speakerphone.

"Smokey, we've got some major problems," said Jason.

"No shit. I know about the Cloud interview and the eight dead men from White Earth. Do you have any other updates for me?"

"Yes, the reporter Cloud met with was dropped off late last night at the Beltrami County Sherriff's office in Bemidji by some military guy. The reporter is still at the Sherriff's office, but the military guy left town after spending the night at the station. I heard the reporter's cousin is a deputy in Beltrami, and he will likely keep the reporter at the office until the feds come in. They could be there already for all I know."

"Anything else?" asked Smokey.

"Yeah. Cloud knew a lot about our operation. He was my right-hand man. Whatever that reporter has on his voice recorder could put us all behind bars for years. The thing that I don't understand is, why were the White Earth thugs there to take him out? How did they know about the interview?"

"That's for me to worry about," growled Smokey.

Smokey had received a call a week earlier from a paid source who watched things closely in Bemidji. The source had been following Cloud and overhead him run his mouth while drinking at the Bemidji Brewery. Cloud bragged about having the Sherriff's department in his pocket after he agreed to an interview with a reporter. Once Smokey had heard this, he hired the men from White Earth – without telling Jason – to kill Cloud and the reporter. He knew that if he had gone straight to Jason with this information, Jason would have just bumped Cloud off, and the reporter would have gone free. The White Earth men were supposed to surveil Cloud, and take him and the reporter out at the first opportune moment. The plan obviously backfired.

"What you have to do now is help me take the reporter down before he runs the interview," said Smokey evenly. "I need you to put some of your best guys on the Sherriff's office. Have them watch the place, and see if they can follow this reporter to whatever safe house the feds take him to. Once they get the exact location, send it to me."

"Not a problem, I'll get you the location soon," said Jason. "What about the military guy?"

"Forget him for now. Focus on the reporter."

"And about the next shipment?"

"We have the product, but we need to wait a week or so to let this all blow over. Be on standby, though. I'll email you the details soon."

"Okay, sounds good. I'll send you the reporter's location as soon as I get it."

Smokey hung up the phone and set it down gently this time on his desk. He crossed his arms and stood up to face his crew.

"Here's the new plan. Once Red Eagle finds the reporter's position, I want Tank to go up and get the tape back."

Smokey looked directly at Tank. "Use whatever means necessary to get it back." Turning back to the others, he added, "While Tank is taking care of them, Jimmy and Marcus will run up the next shipment to the reservations. Jimmy will go up to Red Lake with three kilos, and Marcus will take two kilos up to White Earth. It's by far our biggest and most important shipment yet. We can't screw this up. The shipment will be sometime next week. No mistakes!"

Smokey looked directly into each one of his men's eyes in turn. "We put this all behind us, and then we expand our empire into the Dakotas. Everyone good with the plan?"

Smokey looked first at Marcus.

"Sounds good, boss," said Marcus.

Then Smokey pointed at Jimmy for approval.

"Great plan, Smokey," said Jimmy. "It's smart to have both of us take up different shipments to the reservations to reduce the risk of losing the product."

Smokey looked over at Tank.

"I'm going to kill that reporter slowly. He's going to wish he had never been born once I get through with him."

***

After the meeting, Jimmy drove his Cadillac out to Como Park in Saint Paul. He made several loops around the park to make sure he wasn't being followed. Once he felt safe, he pulled out the phone Agent Sosa had given him. Jimmy typed his message furiously and hit send.

8:21: *Smokey plans to make the dual shipment to the reservations sometime next week. I'm heading up to Red Lake and Marcus is going to White Earth. I'll send specific details closer to the actual exchanges. Also, Smokey wants Tank to kill the reporter, Smith. You may want to keep him somewhere safe.*

Jimmy waited for what seemed like an eternity. Then Sosa replied.

8:29: *Thanks for the update. Continue to keep me posted, and start thinking about white sandy beaches down in the Florida Keys.*

Chapter 15

Bemidji, MN

Agent Sosa finished typing a message on his phone as he walked back into the interrogation room at the Sheriff's department in Bemidji. He tapped Agent Lindberg on the shoulder and showed him the message. Lindberg nodded and left the room. Once the door was closed, Sosa came around the table and stood over me as I sat in an uncomfortable metal chair. I caught a glance at the wall clock: 8:30 am. The DEA arrived, and Sosa and Lindberg interviewed me together for ninety minutes. The next hour was just Lindberg, who was trying to see if I would answer him differently alone. I guess he was playing the good cop role, but it sure didn't feel that way. Now, it was just Sosa standing over me. I felt like I was a terrorist in Guantanamo Bay.

I had been up all night answering questions, and I was exhausted. Before the DEA arrived, Jesse talked to me for several hours, and then the Sheriff came in and did the same. I wondered how Pete was doing; I could hear him in the next room over. It sounded like they were letting him go for the day.

"You jeopardized our entire investigation," Sosa barked. "And more people could have been killed, innocent people. What if your cousin Jesse had been there? He would be lying in a pool of blood right now. How would you explain that to your family?"

"I'm sorry, Sosa. We've been over this already – I know I screwed up by not listening to you."

"You did more than screw up. Eight people are dead! And now what do you think Smokey and his crew will do? I'll tell you what; they'll go into hiding. If they do, we'll be lucky if we ever get within three hundred miles of these guys."

"They can't just leave now," I said. "Based on what Roy Cloud told me last night, they have a huge shipment coming up. They won't flee before they deliver the goods and collect the money. They are sitting on too much heroin."

"Look at you, Mr. Reporter, trying to play detective. They better make that next shipment or you can kiss your fairy tale life goodbye. Do you think your fiancée is going to be happy when you tell her you won't be able to get married because you are sitting in a safe house in the middle of nowhere? Do you think she'll even marry you at all?"

After I called Soojin the night before and told her what had happened, she asked the Governor to see if she could stay in one of his spare bedrooms so she could continue to work on the campaign without being pulled away by authorities. When Sosa found out, he was mad at first, but relented once he realized she was in a secure compound.

"Can I call Soojin?" I asked. "I want to make sure she is still doing all right."

"You better thank me for being such a wonderful human being," said Sosa. "She is absolutely fine. As long as she stays with the Governor, she should be too difficult for one of Smokey's men to approach. You know, if Smokey knows about your relationship, he would love to use her as leverage to get this back." Sosa held up the tape from my voice recorder.

"Hey, that's mine. You can't just take it."

"Like hell I can't. Don't worry, Smith, you'll get it back once we take Smokey and the network down. That way I know you can't run the story before I let you."

"What about freedom of the press?"

Sosa laughed. "Try pulling that card on me, and I'll start to think a lot harder about that time I caught you with Brown Sugar. Would you care to explain that in front of a judge?"

"Just make sure I get the tape back soon. When are we leaving?"

"We are working through the logistics right now. Soon."

"Where are we going?"

"That's not something you need to know now, or even later. We will take all of your electronics and put blindfolds on you. The next thing you see is a house that's somewhere safe."

"How long will we be there?"

"As long as it takes to arrest Smokey and his network. Could be days, weeks, maybe even months."

"They're going to make the shipment soon," I reminded him.

"Let me worry about that. Time to put your blindfold on."

***

I could see out the bottom of my blindfold just enough to know Sosa was placing me into the back of a vehicle. Just before I stepped in, he told me to stop. I heard something jingle, and a moment later I had handcuffs tightly wrapped around my wrists. Sosa grabbed me by the arm and shirt collar and lowered my head into the car. I bumped it against the door on the way in, and Sosa laughed.

"What's so funny?" asked Lindberg.

"Looks like our reporter has a big head," Sosa replied.

Real funny, I thought. They assured me I wasn't under arrest, but that the cuffs were necessary to keep me from pulling off the blindfold. When I asked how long it would be, all I got back was a sarcastic, "It won't be long, Mr. Big Head."

The Crown Victoria took off, and I tried to get comfortable. The cuffs kept cutting into my wrists. I was exhausted, but my mind raced. Was this story worth all this? It certainly wasn't worth Ricky's life. But maybe it would play a part in taking down his killers. I hoped the interview with Cloud gave Sosa and his team enough ammunition to arrest Smokey's whole network. And highlighting the heroin problem in the state could save others from walking down that path. But it was tough to produce a story from the back of a police cruiser.

Just as I was about to fall asleep, Sosa slammed the Crown Victoria into park and said, "We're here."

Chapter 16

Minneapolis, MN

North Minneapolis was notorious for its crime, gang activity, and drugs. Smokey lived right in the center of it all, both in terms of location and the life of misconduct. He had called it home his whole life, and it was where he belonged. With all the money he made from the drug trade, he could afford to live anywhere in the city – but still he chose North Minneapolis.

His home was located on Lyndale Avenue and Twenty-Sixth Avenue on the southwest corner of Farview Park. It was a modest home by drug dealer standards, but it had sentimental value that money couldn't buy. His parents bought it just before he was born. He had spent his entire youth in the house.

While he was locked away in the God-forsaken Stillwater Prison, his parents died in a car crash. They left the house to Smokey in their will. Once Smokey was out of prison, he moved back into his childhood home. It helped ease the pain of missing the last few years of his parents' lives.

It was late at night, but Smokey couldn't sleep. He had too much on his mind. He decided to go for a stroll through the nearby park to get some fresh air and try to clear his head.

Just a little while earlier, Jason Red Eagle had called with an update from one of his guys who had been surveilling the MPR reporter. He was hiding out in a town called Thief River Falls, located in northwest Minnesota. It was actually an ideal location, because it was roughly a little over an hour from both White Earth and Red Lake reservations. He could send all three of his guys up at once, and they would all be close to each other in case something happened. *Nothing is going to happen,* he reassured himself, *but to be safe...*

The park was dead at this late hour except for the occasional homeless person stumbling through, or junkie getting high. Smokey decided to walk all the way to the far end of the park by the athletic field. Back in high school, he had played an instrumental role in helping his football team win the state championship. He was the starting defensive end, and he dominated the line. Plenty of scouts showed up to watch him play, and college football could have been his ticket out of there. He turned down every offer except for the Gophers, at the nearby University of Minnesota. A week before practice started his freshman year, he was caught dealing cocaine. He was immediately kicked off the team and sent straight to the slammer.

That was his first offense, so he wasn't in jail long, but his second visit to the big house was Stillwater. That was after he was caught trying to sell thousands of OxyContin pills. He hated Stillwater worse than anything he had ever encountered. He suffered from claustrophobia, and while he was there he woke up every night with the same nightmare. The walls of his tiny cell closed in slowly, squeezing him to death. During the day, he was so bored he often found himself staring at those same walls for hours on end. His blood boiled every time he heard that name mentioned. *Stillwater was hell.* He was supposed to do five years there, but his parents had called in a favor with a well-respected minister who wrote the judge and had Smokey's sentence dropped to three years. Three months too late to see his parents alive again on the outside. *God rest their souls.*

Smokey came out of prison with new connections and ideas to make money. They were the kind of connections that got you far in the criminal world. He used them to get to Captain, who agreed to supply him with some of the best heroin in the country out of Mexico. The idea to sell to the reservations also came from conversations in prison. It was a good market because of the general hopelessness that came with poverty, driving people to escape through addiction. Smokey knew the feds wouldn't care about the drug problem on the reservations, which would keep him out of trouble. Except, he had a hard time not expanding to other areas of the region because people wanted Brown Sugar.

Just get through this shipment, and North Dakota is yours, he thought. *Build your empire, make your millions, and get out while you can.* That was Smokey's plan, but he had enough self-awareness to realize it would be incredibly hard to stop once he was really rolling in the dough. One thing was certain: he sure as hell was not going back to Stillwater.

Chapter 17

Thief River Falls, MN

It took me several days to figure out where the safe house was located. Rotating local police officers watched the house around the clock, but they were in unmarked squad cars. Then, one of the officers who brought me Dairy Queen one day accidently left the receipt in the bag. I was in Thief River Falls, or at least near there.

I should have known too, as I saw people in the adjacent homes wearing Arctic Cat and Digi-Key shirts to and from work. I must have been close to the factories. I was in a rundown trailer house, on the back corner cul-de-sac of a trailer park. I could count several dozen other trailer houses crammed together on the little street, but wasn't sure as to the full extent the park's size.

Agent Sosa stopped by twice, but he was keeping his cards close to his chest in terms of when it would be safe for me to leave. He said he contacted my boss and family, so they were aware of the situation. I can only imagine how the conversation between him and Bill Anderson went.

I had been at the safe house for six days now and I was going stir crazy. I was completely cut off from the outside world with no electronics. For a news junkie, I was going through withdrawal. My one consolation was knowing Soojin was safe. She had worked so hard on the Governor's campaign that I would have been devastated if she were pulled from it. Now, my biggest worry was trying to get out of this safe house so I could get back to Saint Paul to marry her.

On the seventh day, a Saturday, I was just getting my daily fast-food lunch from the city police officer when Agent Lindberg showed up. He looked excited about something, and in a hurry. He motioned for me to sit down at the table. "Cooper, I trust you've had a pleasant stay at our fine safe house thus far," said Lindberg, "but, it should be coming to an end soon."

"You're taking down Smokey and his crew," I said.

"We are going to get them tonight if all goes as planned. If we're successful, you can leave tomorrow morning."

"Where is Agent Sosa?" I asked.

"He's back in Minneapolis."

"He's going to bust Smokey himself?"

"Yes, and we have simultaneous operations in four other locations as well," said Lindberg.

"Let me guess," I said. "Red Lake, White Earth, Chicago, and… what's the fourth?"

"Oh, that's right, Detective Smith," Lindberg said mockingly. "You were correct on the first three locations. The fourth spot is right here."

"Here?" I repeated. "Is there a connection to this town I'm missing?"

"Yes, it's you. We have information that suggests Smokey's muscle man, Tank, will be looking for you tonight, here in TRF, as the locals call it. We want to arrest him when he gets to town, so I'll be staying here tonight."

"Am I safe?" Worry made my voice rise a notch.

"We have city, county, state, and federal law enforcement officers already in position in all four locations, including here. There's nothing to worry about," said Lindberg.

"Yeah, but I've heard Tank is massive. If he gets to me, I'm dead."

"Just relax. Sit back and enjoy your last wonderful evening in the Countryside Trailer Court. Oh, and there's one more thing. Sosa asked me to return this to you; he said you might need it soon."

Lindberg reached into his pocket and handed me back my tape from the interview with Roy Cloud.

"We, of course, made copies of it so it can be used in court," said Lindberg. "This is the original though, just for you."

"Thanks," I said sarcastically. "That was so thoughtful of you."

***

The rest of the day dragged on. I tried to distract myself, but it was useless. I knew if Tank were going to attack me, it would be after dark. The sun was setting and I was restless. I wished I could be on the move, as I felt like a sitting duck. To feel like I was doing something, I decided to stay on watch all night, looking out from different windows in the trailer to see if anyone was approaching. I wasn't armed, so there wasn't much I could do except call out to Lindberg, whose unmarked Crown Victoria was parked in front of our trailer.

The clock on the wall now read 10:37 pm, and I was getting tired. I decided to make the rounds again to stay awake. I looked out the back window and saw a uniformed police officer on foot patrol. I was glad there was a second officer nearby. Beyond him all I could see were a couple trees, a big, open field behind them in the darkness – nothing out there for miles. Out the side windows, all I could see were the adjacent trailer houses. The one to the east of us was completely dark, but in the one to the west I could make out a man in the living room illuminated by the glow of his television. *What was he watching?* Whatever it was, things were about to get more interesting right here than anything he could find on TV.

I went up to the front window and saw Lindberg still sitting there. He was illuminated by his smart phone. He was probably getting the play-by-play from his DEA colleagues who were likely already making arrests. After a few minutes, I saw Lindberg drink the last drop of his coffee and get out of the car. I peered out the corner of the window so he couldn't see me. *Where is he going? What is he doing? Oh, God, really? He's going to urinate on the side of my trailer house with only a thin sheet of metal and some insulation between him and me? I guess it's better than him coming inside every thirty minutes.*

Just as I turned to start my window rotations over, I saw a large shadow moving fast in the dark toward Lindberg, who was still draining his bladder. It took my brain an extra second to process what was happening when Tank sent a massive elbow down on the back of Lindberg's head. Lindberg's body fell limp. By this point, I had completely opened the window shade and Tank looked up at me with a killer's gaze.

We locked eyes for what felt like three whole seconds, and then we both sprinted. Tank was headed toward the front door, while I rushed to the bedroom.

I blew open the bedroom door and darted to the window and opened it, just like I had rehearsed. I heard loud bangs on the front door, and then the lock gave and the door was open. Tank was inside. He started to dash toward the back just as I slipped down outside. I raced around the house, tripping over a body lying behind the trailer. It was a police officer – Tank must have knocked him out first.

Once I reached the front of the house, I saw that Lindberg's car door was open, and I jumped into the driver's seat. I fumbled with the keys that were dangling from the ignition and started the car. I tried to put it into drive, but my adrenaline was pumping, and I accidently put it in reverse. I slammed the Crown Victoria back into the trailer house just as Tank was coming out.

I finally found drive as Tank descended on me. He slammed into my driver's side door, jarring the vehicle. I lunged forward, but there was a truck coming into the cul-de-sac right in front me. I had to swerve to avoid it, but it nearly took out Tank as the driver hit the brakes.

I watched in my rearview mirror in horror as Tank ripped the driver from the truck and jumped in. I drove straight, but missed the turn for the exit. I wound up in another cul-de-sac and was forced to double back. I made the correct turn this time just as Tank caught up to me. He tried to ram into me and narrowly missed.

I had never been to TRF, but I knew my best bet was to head toward the downtown area – that was where I would most likely find a police station or other sort of help. But where was downtown? I headed east out of the trailer park, but turned right immediately because I saw bright lights. Tank was a few hundred meters behind me, but his truck didn't have the acceleration power of the Crown Victoria.

I was now headed south on a straight road, and I could see the lights on my left were from the Arctic Cat and Digi-Key factories. Beyond them was darkness – the countryside. Not good. I turned left at the next road and was heading east again. I could see a stop light ahead. The road sign read *Highway 32*. I turned left onto it at the stoplight, heading northeast. Tank was still on my heels, and he had his hand out of the window.

Glass splintered as a bullet hit my rear window. It must have been bullet proof. All I could do now was to outrun him.

I zipped past the DQ that had kept my belly full all week and sped toward the town's lights. I was doing 85 mph in a 30 mph zone as I passed residential housing and an empty gas station named *Pennington Main*. Tank was charging fast behind me as I headed straight north through the town.

Then, I spotted it. On my left was the TRF police station. There were two city police officers idling in their cars on the street as we zoomed by. They instantly turned on their lights and sirens and gave chase. I went a few more blocks and made a quick turn right hoping Tank would skid forward so the cops could close on him. He made a miraculous turn with the truck, and stuck with me.

I was now heading east again, and I started to increase my speed as I crossed a bridge over a river. The road now had double lanes on it, and Tank managed to creep up next to me. I could still see the police cruisers behind, and another cop approached me straight ahead from the opposite direction. Tank tried slamming into my vehicle, but I accelerated past him. He tried again as the road started to veer to the right, and he clipped my back bumper. I started to fish-tail, and I had trouble getting the car back under control. The approaching police officer had turned across into our lane and was blocking the road in front of us. I managed to slow my speed to avoid smashing into the police cruiser, but the wheels turned too sharply and I ended up getting stuck sideways in the median against a tree.

I looked back and saw Tank smash directly into the police car. The collision knocked the police cruiser back, and it slid with the momentum of the truck. Tank then put his truck in reverse and came back toward me.

I tumbled out of my vehicle and started running north just as Tank and the two trailing police officers made it to the Crown Victoria. There was another crash as both police cars collided with Tank's truck. I looked over my shoulder as I ran. Tank had managed to get out of his truck, and was behind me on foot now, with the two police officers tailing him.

I was in a dark residential area, but it looked as though it opened up ahead and dipped down a hill. I heard the police officers yelling for Tank to stop as they followed. I started running down the hill into a park, but as I got halfway there I realized it was a dead end – a sandy beach area opened below, giving way to a river.

There's no way that big moose can swim, I thought.

I rushed down to the beach and saw Tank was closing on me, but the two police officers were also still in pursuit. I sprinted as far out as I could in the water and then dove headfirst into the river as I heard gunshots. I was a strong swimmer, and didn't stop until I reached the other shore a hundred meters away. I pulled myself up and looked back across the river.

Tank remained on the beach, down on one knee and clutching his side. He was likely hit by one of the officers' bullets, but I couldn't tell how badly. The two officers descended on him and he spun around, lunging at them with whatever reserve he had left. He tackled one to the ground, but the other officer pulled out what must have been a Taser, because in moments Tank shook violently and then collapsed.

I breathed a huge sigh of relief, reminding myself to thank my parents for putting me into swimming lessons when I was a kid.

Chapter 18

Minneapolis, MN

Agent Sosa was set up across the street from Smokey's house in a van disguised as a maintenance vehicle. The house was old, with two stories and a stone walkway that led up from the sidewalk to a small enclosed patio area at the entrance of the home. He had been watching and waiting for Smokey since 4:12 pm. Toothpick had said Smokey would be in close communication with him and the team all night from his home office.

It was now 8:30 pm, and Sosa had yet to see a sign of Smokey. *He must be in there; where else would he be?* he asked himself. Once the arrests of Smokey's men were confirmed up north, a team of DEA agents would take down Captain in Chicago, and Sosa and his team would detain Smokey. Waiting was always the hardest part of this game, and Sosa requested updates constantly from his team. Toothpick said the exchanges would likely happen between 10 and 10:30 pm. Sosa and his colleagues would be ready.

***

Smokey was away from home all afternoon running errands when one of his neighbors told him there was a suspicious van parked in front of his house at 5:17 pm. People in North Minneapolis took care of each other when it came to the police, and Smokey knew right away he was in trouble. He had a bad feeling about tonight, anyway, and the suspicious van confirmed it.

He decided to play it safe and prepare for an immediate departure out of the country. He had planned months ahead for this, and went straight to his storage unit in Richfield just off of I-494.

Smokey had rented a large unit the size of a one-stall garage with a fake driver's license the previous year. His locker contained a pre-packed suitcase with disguises, wigs, dress clothes, and money. He also had an alias driver's license, passport, credit card, and burner phone. He put a tear-away mustache on, and then added old reading glasses. He changed into some plain dress clothes and was instantly transformed from a thug of the streets of North Minneapolis to a professor in the classrooms of Saint Paul's Universities. He checked himself over in his rear view mirror, then ditched his vehicle at the storage locker and caught a cab to the Minneapolis-Saint Paul Airport.

***

There was a seat available on a late-night flight from Minneapolis to Cancun, Mexico. Smokey bought a last-minute ticket and paid for it in cash using the name Robert Church. He would go to the terminal to wait for word from his men. If all went as planned, he would casually leave the airport and find a safe place to stay the night. He would only be out a thousand dollars for the flight – well worth it for the peace of mind. If things went sour with his team, he could board the plane as scheduled and fly down to Cancun. From there, he could go anywhere in Mexico or Latin America. Maybe he could strike up a relationship with one of the cartels directly and double his profits in future drug ventures.

Smokey made it through the security gate fine, but then had to go through the dreaded passport control. Smokey's fake passport was one of the best – he had paid

$3,000 to a professional who guaranteed his product. Despite his size, Smokey's professorial look helped him go unnoticed in the airport. He handed his passport to the Customs and Border Patrol officer. The officer studied it over, a little longer than Smokey thought was required. *Come on, buddy, just let me through.*

The officer looked up from the passport and asked, "Are you going to Cancun for vacation, Mr. Church?"

"Yes, sir," Smokey answered.

"Huh. Well, you don't seemed dressed for it," said the officer.

"Oh, I came right from work. I planned to change as soon as we land."

The officer looked somewhat skeptical. "Mr. Church, can you please look into the camera for a picture, and then place your fingers on the scanner so we can get a biometrics reading?"

"Sure, no problem, officer," said Smokey. He was starting to sweat a little now. The fake passport had held up, but how quickly would the biometrics link Robert Church to Tyrone Carter? Smokey hoped it wasn't anytime soon.

"Thanks, Mr. Church. Have a nice trip."

***

Agent Sosa received a message at 10:20 pm that Marcus and Jimmy had both been arrested up on the reservations. That was Sosa's cue to strike. He called the raid team from around the block and they all swarmed in on Smokey's house. They knocked down doors and threw flash bangs. They methodically cleared each room looking for Smokey. He wasn't there. *You've got to be kidding me.*

As Sosa exited the house, his phone rang. He was getting a call from the U.S. Customs and Border Patrol at the MSP airport. He had the number preprogrammed on his phone because they called him with tips on people the DEA had watchlisted for travel.

"Agent Sosa, this is Officer Clark at MSP. Twenty minutes ago we had a hit on someone you watchlisted as an immediate 24/7 call to your cell phone. His name is Tyrone Carter of North Minneapolis. He's using the alias Robert Church and he's trying to get on a plane for Cancun in thirty minutes."

"Officer Clark, can you stall the plane? We are about twenty minutes from MSP. We are coming right now."

"Roger that, we have men at the gate, but they haven't spotted him yet. We will keep looking though and let you know."

"What are the flight, terminal, and gate numbers?"

"It's a Sun Country flight, 581 out of the Humphrey Terminal, gate H1."

"Got it, we'll be right there."

***

It was 10:45 pm, and Smokey was fidgeting with his boarding pass, folding and unfolding it. He hadn't heard anything from Jimmy or Marcus yet. But his 11 pm flight had been delayed for mechanical reasons, so he could wait a little longer for updates. His phone started vibrating in his pocket, and Smokey saw it was Tank. He accepted the call. Tank was breathing heavily, and there was a loud noise of an engine churning, with a faint sound of sirens in the background.

"Smokey, Smokey, are you there?" Tank called out.

"Yes, what's going on?"

"I'm in a vehicle pursuit of the reporter right now, but I may be in trouble. I have two cops on my tail."

"What? What happened?" Smokey demanded.

"Boss, I can't really talk right now, but I took out a couple of cops at the house, and the reporter bolted to the cop's car. I've been chasing him for a little bit and picked up a couple of other cops in the process."

"You need to take care of this," Smokey said through gritted teeth. "Right now."

"I will, boss – I have to go, though," Tank said.

Smokey heard the phone drop, along with the acceleration of Tank's vehicle, followed by squealing tires and a crash. A gear shift, another crash. Approaching sirens, men yelling. Then silence. Smokey strained to listen, and thought he heard gunshots. Then the call dropped.

Dammit! They got Tank. No matter what, now he had to get on that plane. He rushed down the H Concourse toward H1, but as he passed gate H4, he saw two officers standing in front of his gate. Smokey's stomach plummeted.

He quickly turned and headed back toward the terminal exit. He moved with the same brisk walk as most other visitors to the airport; he avoided running so he would not draw attention to himself. Smokey stepped out of the airport and on to the street just as two dark Crown Victorias and a Suburban came screaming to halt at the next terminal exit to his left. Feds poured out of the vehicles. He ran.

***

Agent Sosa jumped out of his Crown Victoria and spotted Smokey ahead at the next terminal exit door. *You're mine.* Sosa gave chase as Smokey bolted back inside the terminal and clambered up the escalator, knocking aside weary travelers as he went. Sosa followed him up the escalator, across the skywalk, and through the parking terminal to the Humphrey Light Rail Station.

Smokey was fast, but Sosa held with him. Sosa's men were lagging behind as a light rail car pulled up ahead of them and opened its doors. Smokey seemed to increase his speed, and he made it through the last set of open doors. The lights started to flash, and the doors were about to close. Sosa sprinted and lunged with all his strength, making it into the car as the doors closed. No one on his team had managed to keep up throughout the whole chase.

Smokey was heading away from Sosa down the car when he reversed direction and came right at him. With bystanders on board, Sosa couldn't risk shooting at Smokey. Instead, he met him with a kick to the face. Smokey took the kick and followed through with a spear that pelted Sosa to the floor. Sosa blacked out for a second, then managed to throw an elbow up that connected on Smokey's jaw.

Smokey turned his head to the side, but he had at least a hundred pounds on Sosa, so he leaned his weight on him as he reached for Sosa's firearm. Sosa wiggled his arm free and punched Smokey in the throat. Smokey fell back gasping for air, but quickly got to his feet. He threw a slow roundhouse punch that would have knocked Sosa out cold had it connected. Instead, Sosa ducked the punch and came up to elbow Smokey in the ear with all his force.

Smokey fell to his knees. Sosa jumped on his back and started throwing punches to the back of Smokey's head. Smokey put his massive hands behind his head for protection and slid away. The light rail car stopped at the American Blvd Station. That was when Smokey made a fatal decision. Even though his size gave him an advantage on the compact light rail car, he bolted out the door into the night. The rail station was dead, and he and Sosa were the only ones to get out.

Sosa drew his handgun and yelled for Smokey to stop. Smokey sprinted across the road as Sosa pulled the trigger. The round entered Smokey's left calf, and he keeled over. He stumbled when he tried to get up to run. Sosa swooped in on him and pointed the gun right in his face.

"Turn around and put your face on the ground!"

"Shoot me! Kill me now!"

"Get your face in the ground!"

"I'm not going back to Stillwater," Smokey said. "Kill me." Smokey made a weak lunge for Sosa.

Sosa slid out of the way, smacking Smokey in the back of the head with the butt of his gun. The blow combined with Smokey's body momentum resulted in a hard crash onto the pavement. Sosa quickly pinned Smokey's head to the gravel with his knee and handcuffed him.

"Smokey, you're under arrest – and your old friend Mr. Stillwater just might be calling your name."

Smokey flexed his muscles, closed his eyes, and clenched his teeth. Then he let out a bellowing roar of defeat. He knew he was going to spend the rest of his days in Stillwater, and that was worse to him than death.

Chapter 19

Twin Cities, MN

The press conference was scheduled to begin in a few minutes at 11 am in the DEA's federal office building on Washington Avenue in Minneapolis. I had talked to Agent Sosa the day before on the long car ride back to the Twin Cities, and he said MPR could air the story as soon as the press conference finished. He even agreed to give me a few voice-recorded quotes that no other news outlet would get.

I called Bill Anderson next at his house and told him everything that had transpired. He assembled a media team to work all Sunday night and into Monday morning to prepare our piece so it was ready to air immediately following the press conference. Bill was able to get a five-part, running special on the popular *Minnesota News Presents* show from noon to 1 pm, Monday through Friday. The timing of the first show would be perfectly synced with the end of today's press conference, which MPR planned to stream live.

***

My microphone was on the podium, and my recorder was already turned on when Agent Sosa walked into the press conference with several other federal agents and representatives from the U.S. Attorney's office. Sosa pulled out a piece of paper with his official remarks and set it on the podium. He looked out on all the media gathered in the room and saw me sitting in the middle of the pack. He flashed me a smile, then read:

"We set out to stop the flow of heroin to reservations in Minnesota, and we are pleased to announce the indictment of thirty-two members of a multi-state heroin trafficking conspiracy. The network was led by Tyrone 'Smokey' Carter out of North Minneapolis. Our goal, however, was not just to take down the head of the organization, or the people bringing the heroin into the state of Minnesota. We wanted to make it as difficult as possible for someone to come in and pick up where this organization left off."

"The indictment of the Carter drug trafficking organization is emblematic of our commitment to combatting heroin trafficking in Minnesota. These defendants, led by Carter, represented the most significant source of heroin in Indian Country. Through close collaboration with law enforcement at all levels, we have officially shut down this major pipeline that was spreading heroin across the Red Lake and White Earth Indian Reservations and the surrounding communities."

Sosa paused and looked out at the gathered crowd.

"Carter cared nothing about the collateral damage the drugs inflicted upon neighborhoods, families, and especially young children on tribal lands in Minnesota and throughout the north region. With this successful take down, we have sent a clear message to drug trafficking organizations that drugs will not be tolerated on or near reservations. I think we've also proved today that criminals like Carter have always been and will always be on the wrong side of history, and now they know it."

"Any Questions?"

As the other reporters asked questions, my thoughts drifted over the past few weeks. I finally had this story as a feather in my hat – but I no longer had my friend, Ricky. Did I do enough to avenge his death? Would my story prevent others from walking down the same path? The press conference closed up right at noon. I had already returned to Wellstone a few minutes earlier.

I turned on the radio, forever set to 91.1 FM, just in time for my special to begin.

This is the story of an epidemic drug – heroin – *that plagues our great state. On today's Minnesota News Presents, we begin the first of a five-day series titled 'Brown Sugar in Minnesota,' reported by* MPR*'s Cooper Smith*…

***

I inched along I-94, headed east for Saint Paul. Traffic was heavy, but I didn't mind. I parked a few blocks away from work and listened to the last five minutes of the special.

My first major story. Always the toughest to get, they say. Who knows, maybe this one could even win the Peabody... Okay, don't get too ahead of yourself. I hoped this story would at least protect my job for a while at MPR. And, who knows, maybe I could give Lisa Larson a run for her money at the investigative team.

I walked down Cedar Street, and as I approached MPR headquarters I could see Bill Anderson looking out of his office window on the third floor, grinning at a gaggle of reporters from all the Twin Cities majors including the *Star Tribune, Pioneer Press, Kare11,* and *Fox9.*

They all stood outside on the street looking up at the news ticker. I knew they were waiting for me to return so they could ask questions about my sources and other angles. I slid around them as they tried to mob me and said, "No comment."

From the window above, Bill flashed me a huge smile and a thumbs-up. *Now I know I've made it.*

I stopped in the center of Cedar Street for my daily moment of Zen and looked up at the news ticker.

> *Monday, August 25, 2014 –*
> *Listen in Each Day at Noon to*
> *Hear the Story of Brown Sugar*
> *in Minnesota...*

I looked back up at Bill and smiled. I returned his thumbs up and entered the building with my head held a little higher than ever before.

Chapter 20

Over the Atlantic Ocean

"Do you Cooper Smith take Soojin Kim to be your wife?"
"I do."

Everything after those two words was a blur. I worked every night and weekend with Soojin on Governor Knutson's campaign. On Election Day, he won re-election with just over fifty percent of the vote.

The very next day, Soojin and I were on a flight heading east across the big pond for a much-needed European honeymoon. Just as I was about to fall asleep, Soojin leaned over and said, "You know, the next time you are in a safe house, and a guy who goes by 'Tank' is after you ..." Soojin paused. "You might want to call me in to be your body guard."

I smiled. "That's a good idea Mrs. Smith. I didn't realize they taught you how to deal with a scenario like that in Taekwondo."

"Mrs. Smith still sounds so funny to me. I guess it will take a while to get used to." Soojin laughed.

"So, I guess now would be the best time to tell you."
"Tell me what?"

"Right before I left work yesterday, Bill called me into his office."

"What did he say?"

"He told me my job was secure for a while following the success of the Brown Sugar story. He also said he was sending me on a 'special' assignment to one of the most dangerous places in the world as soon as we return from our honeymoon."

Soojin turned to face me. "Really? I'll start naming places and you nod once I've guessed correctly."

"Okay, go."

"Syria, Iraq, Yemen, Afghanistan, Iran, North Korea…"

I shook my head at all of her guesses. Then, with a straight face, I said, "Actually it's more dangerous than all of those places combined – and it's right here in America."

"Where is it?"

"North Dakota," I replied. "The rough and tumble oil fields of western North Dakota."

Acknowledgments

This book would not have been possible without the support and encouragement from my family and friends. Also, words cannot express my gratitude to editor Lacey Louwagie for her professional advice and assistance in polishing this manuscript. Although the final editorial decisions are all my own, Lacey provided valuable guidance. Lastly, thanks to the special people of Minnesota for making our home the greatest state in all the land.

About the Author

Joe Field is a thriller writer whose debut book, Brown Sugar in Minnesota, features Minnesota Public Radio reporter Cooper Smith. Field is a Minnesota native, and is a member of the International Thriller Writers. Subscribe to email alerts on Field's website, and connect on Amazon and Goodreads.

joefield.net
amazon.com/author/joefield
goodreads.com/joefield

If you enjoyed Brown Sugar in Minnesota, please check out

BLACK GOLD IN NORTH DAKOTA

COOPER SMITH BOOK 2

Made in the USA
Middletown, DE
12 June 2016